Our favorite New England small town attorney-turned-sleuth Gaby Quinn is at it again in Andrea O'Connor's expertly drawn novel, *9 Donovan's Way*. Quinn, who we initially met in O'Connor's first Woodson Falls novel, *16 Lakeview Terrace*, is a plucky and likable attorney with a nose for detail—details that grippingly add up to a shocking crime. O'Connor, as in her first novel, brings the town of Woodson Falls and all of its inhabitants to life with her own nose for detail and shows, once again, a mastery of the book's subject.

— Don Lowe, First Selectman, Sherman, CT

After reading Andrea O'Connor's first book, *Woodson Falls: 16 Lakeview Terrace*, I was looking forward to the next mystery in the series, and I wasn't disappointed. Gaby Quinn, the main character, has a habit of getting into the middle of things without really trying. Going about her day-to-day work as a probate attorney should have been one boring day after another of shuffling paperwork. Somehow a dark cloud follows her around and a week or two of billable hours turns into one strange twist after another. The characters come to life and the town and events are real, strange, but real. After the first few pages, I couldn't put it down. A great read and I am looking forward to the next book, *Woodson Falls: 2 Sunrise Trail*. What other strange events will happen in this small affluent community?

— Marc Youngquist, author of the *Maidstone* mysteries

A cozy mystery for readers who think they don't like cozy mysteries! I enjoyed the first book in the series and patiently waited for this second installment. *Woodson Falls: 9 Donovan's Way* does not disappoint. I loved learning more about Gaby and the town of Woodson Falls. I'm invested in Gaby's backstory and impressed with her character. I think the legal angle is brilliantly done. Who knew that estate law mysteries could be so compelling! I can't wait for Gaby's next case!

—Brandy Gray, NetGalley reviewer

This is the second book in the Gaby Quinn Mystery series, and the second I've read set in Woodson Falls. Another good mystery told from the viewpoint of Gaby Quinn, the local attorney. The character development and clues are spot on—and it's good to see Gaby's relationships, particularly with Matt and Nell, developing; and her own character building and becoming stronger and more confident. This story focuses on the mysterious death of an author and the disappearance of his girlfriend, but there are side issues dealt with as well along the way, all of which add to the rounding out of the town, its residents and its problems. The end of the book gives us a tantalizing glimpse into the focus of the next story. I'm looking forward to it and hoping that the series continues as I am now very much invested in these characters.

— **Barbara Crompton, NetGalley reviewer**

Woodson Falls: 9 Donovan's Way

A Gaby Quinn Mystery

OTHER BOOKS BY THE AUTHOR

The Gaby Quinn Mystery Series
WOODSON FALLS: 16 LAKEVIEW TERRACE
WOODSON FALLS: 9 DONOVAN'S WAY
WOODSON FALLS: 2 SUNRISE TRAIL *(coming soon)*

Woodson Falls:
9 Donovan's Way

A Gaby Quinn Mystery

by
Andrea O'Connor

*Enjoy your visit to
Woodson Falls*

Andrea O'Connor

EMERALD LAKE
BOOKS
Sherman, Connecticut

Books published by Emerald Lake Books may be ordered through your favorite booksellers or by visiting emeraldlakebooks.com.

Library of Congress Cataloging-in-Publication Data

Names: O'Connor, Andrea B., author.

Title: Woodson Falls : 9 Donovan's Way / Andrea O'Connor.

Description: Sherman, Connecticut : Emerald Lake Books, [2021] | Series: A Gaby Quinn mystery ; 2 | Summary: "Attorney Gaby Quinn has settled into her law practice in the small Connecticut town of Woodson Falls. She's quietly rebuilding her life after the tragic murder of her husband in New York City. When famous author Phillip Mitchell suddenly dies of an apparent heart attack, his ex-wife asks Gaby to handle the estate. Everything seems above board until some things turn up missing, including Mitchell's girlfriend"-- Provided by publisher.

Identifiers: LCCN 2021004826 (print) | LCCN 2021004827 (ebook) | ISBN 9781945847417 (paperback) | ISBN 9781945847424 (epub)

Subjects: GSAFD: Mystery fiction.

Classification: LCC PS3615.C5843 W63 2021 (print) | LCC PS3615.C5843 (ebook) | DDC 813/.6--dc23

LC record available at https://lccn.loc.gov/2021004826

LC ebook record available at https://lccn.loc.gov/2021004827

*In memory of Gertrude Conlon, who nurtured my writing,
giving me my first Roget's Thesaurus way back in 1959,
inscribed "To help you find the right word."*

And always John, for all you've given me.

Prologue

THE TELEPHONE IN THE DOWNSTAIRS BEDROOM rang insistently. Phillip Mitchell was tempted to ignore it. He would usually just let calls go to voicemail, the messages to be picked up later when he could respond—or not.

He stood in the bedroom doorway, staring at the lake, visible through the kitchen window opposite him. The view from his office was so much better. He picked up the phone, interrupting its ring.

"Yes?" he said gruffly to his caller.

"Oh dear, love," said the woman at the other end of the line, her voice tinged with a faint French accent. "I've disturbed your work."

"No, no, Danielle. Never. Are you okay? The baby?"

"Everything's fine, my dear one. No problems. It's just that I'm mapping out a new tour my agency may offer in the coming season. The tour would be in and around Saratoga Springs. I thought I'd drive down from Quebec on Friday, check out the sights, restaurants, hotels. It's just a short drive from there to Woodson Falls, and I wondered if you'd have time for a quick visit over the weekend? I'd have to leave on Monday, but it would be so very good to see you."

"Oh, sweetheart! That would be wonderful! Beyond wonderful! The only wrinkle is that Alan has me scheduled to speak about my new novel at some college in Pennsylvania—in Scranton, I think—Friday evening. It's too late to cancel. I'll have to stay for dinner and was planning to spend the night there and drive back to Woodson Falls Saturday morning. That would shorten our time together, but I so want to see you. Even for a short time."

"Great. I can book into one of the hotels I'm considering for the tour, stay there Friday night, and head down to Connecticut on Saturday to meet you at the cottage."

"Why spend money on a hotel? Drive down when you're done with your exploration of Saratoga Springs and stay at my place Friday night. You know where the key is."

"I don't want to intrude…"

"Don't be foolish. Any time you want to spend here is just fine with me. Better than fine… I love you."

"I love you, too. Well then, that's settled."

"And Danielle. Don't worry about our baby. I've told Alan about the pregnancy. I wanted to warn him I would be taking a break from writing when this next book is done—probably a long break."

"Really? I'm thrilled you're thinking that way. But how did Alan take the news?"

"Badly, I fear. But he'll get over it. It really doesn't matter what Alan thinks. I want to be fully present for you and our baby."

"You seemed so upset when I told you I was pregnant. Really. I can manage raising this child myself."

"I know I wasn't exactly thrilled at first when you told me the news just before Christmas, but now… I've embraced the idea of fatherhood and want to enjoy it with you. I missed a lot of that with Tim. Eleanora insisted on a full-time nanny until he was in nursery school so she could focus on her business. Then she pushed hard for him to be sent to boarding school. It's only recently that I've had the chance to get close to him. I don't want to throw away this second chance. And besides… Oh, Danielle, do you know how very much I love you?"

Chapter 1

GABY WAS SIPPING HER COFFEE and leafing through the local paper when Emma Larson came over from the deli with Gaby's buttered roll.

"Have you heard the latest?" asked the bubbly blonde, wife of the owner of Mike's Place, the only grocery store in Woodson Falls.

Gaby smiled at her friend. "Probably not. What's up?"

Emma sat down beside Gaby. Mike's Place offered a gathering space next to the deli where customers could linger with coffee or a sandwich.

"You know Phillip Mitchell? Lives in one of those old cottages on Woodson Lake?"

"I've met him a few times at the Sail Club. What about him?"

"Well, he's just about the most famous person in Woodson Falls. Or was... He's dead!"

"What?"

"Yes! Totally unexpected! Mike was one of the EMTs on the call. I liked the man. I mean, he was always friendly—well, sometimes a bit too friendly. He was an unabashed flirt and a bit eccentric but always pleasant."

Mitchell had called 911 claiming he was having severe chest pain and thought he might be having another heart attack. He'd had two in the past and knew the symptoms. When the ambulance arrived a mere fifteen minutes later, the EMTs found the sixty-two-year-old Mitchell unresponsive, with no pulse or discernible respirations. They began CPR and continued their resuscitation efforts on the way to Prescott Memorial Hospital, where he was pronounced dead.

"Maybe you'll get the case," Emma continued. "After all, you must be Woodson Falls' most famous lawyer after that case up on Lakeview Terrace, and it *is* the kind of work you do."

"More like Woodson Falls' only lawyer," Gaby replied with a smile, "though I do a good deal of probate work. It's more likely the family will contact whoever drafted Mitchell's will if he had one."

"Still, it would be fascinating to deal with the estate of such a famous author," Emma declared before getting up to serve a customer.

Phillip Mitchell was the successful author of several novels set in the French and Indian Wars of the mid-1700s. Fashioned as biographies, Mitchell's engaging writing style had enabled the novels to capture a fairly large share of the historical fiction niche. His own experiences in the Vietnam War, where he lost the lower half of his left leg as well as his right eye, provided realistic color to his writing.

The man posed a dashing figure. A flashy dresser, even in rural Woodson Falls, Mitchell was often seen sporting a scarf at the neck of his safari jacket and wearing his trademark fedora whenever he was out and about. He kept his salt-and-pepper beard neatly trimmed, while his waxed handlebar mustache reflected his quick and easy smile. The simple black patch worn over his right eye lent an air of mystery to the well-built man.

Mitchell's ex-wife Eleanora was an equally successful design consultant with a large New York City-based business she managed from their well-appointed apartment on Central Park West. Tall, elegant and startlingly attractive as a young woman, the years hadn't been kind to Eleanora, who had packed on pounds despite her daily workouts with a personal trainer. Her scalp was visible through a dwindling head of frequently dyed hair that had turned an unattractive pink.

Once they each had achieved a measure of financial success, Phillip and Eleanora had purchased and renovated one of the old cottages comprising Donovan's Camp, a cluster of fishing shacks arrayed along the southern shore of Woodson Lake. Over the years, New Yorkers seeking refuge from hectic city life had bought up most of the shacks. They poured money into the structures, transforming them into small but charming year-round dwellings suitable for a weekend escape.

Although they'd enjoyed a happy marriage in their early years together, the couple began to bicker once their only child Timothy was sent off to boarding school. Their weekend tirades, in which Eleanora accused Phillip of various infidelities, echoed across Woodson Lake, punctuating the usual quiet of the sleepy country town. When the couple finally called it quits, Eleanora kept the New York apartment. Phillip stayed on at the Woodson Falls cottage, turning their large bedroom with its fabulous view of the lake and the falls beyond into a writer's retreat.

Arriving home to her cottage on Beaver Trail, Gaby unloaded the supplies and equipment she had picked up at Frank's Supply Depot. Spring had finally asserted itself in the past few days, and she wanted to get a head start on restoring the rambling garden her grandparents had maintained so many years ago. She had renovated the cottage she inherited from her grandfather before moving to Woodson Falls from New York following her young husband's violent death. But she had found little time or energy to engage in the significant work involved in bringing the sprawling garden back to life. She had resolved to tackle the work this year as an antidote to the grief that sometimes overwhelmed her still.

Putting everything into the garage, she entered the house and was immediately greeted by Katrina, her German Sheprador companion. Acquired as an emotional support dog that had gotten Gaby through some difficult episodes of PTSD, Kat had become a fixture in Gaby's life.

Letting the dog out the door, Gaby picked up the ringing phone. "Law offices, Gabriella Quinn speaking," she announced.

"Eleanora Mitchell calling. My ex-husband, Phillip Mitchell, died last Thursday. I called the probate court in Prescott this morning, and Judge Taylor suggested you as an attorney who might handle the estate since Mitch was a resident of Woodson Falls. I'm much too busy with my design business here in New York City to become involved with this. Our son, Timothy, is a sophomore at Harvard up in Cambridge and in no position to take this on. I'm sure Mitch would have wanted Timothy to be the executor as well as the beneficiary of his estate."

Gaby had the urge to say "Whoa! You don't get to decide" but heard her caller out instead. Ten minutes later, Eleanora had run out of steam.

"I just heard about Mr. Mitchell's death. I'm so sorry for your loss. Do you know if your ex-husband had a will?" she asked. "That would name his preference for the executor of his estate as well as his beneficiaries."

Her question only wound Eleanora up again.

"Well, *of course*, Mitch would have named Timothy as executor. Who else would he name? But as I've said, neither Timothy nor I have the time to manage Mitch's affairs. Would you take this on? I'd like this matter settled as quickly as possible. Mitch was supporting our son's education, and Timothy needs any inheritance he might receive to pay for his studies at Harvard. Not at all inexpensive, you know."

"I'd be happy to help, as long as the individual named to administer the estate decides to retain my services. The first step would be to determine whether Mr. Mitchell left a will."

"I was at the cottage right after Mitch died. I had to come up to Connecticut to identify the body and make the necessary arrangements. Mitch named his brother Bill as his primary emergency contact the last time he was in the hospital, but he left my name as his second-ary contact and never changed it. Bill was out of town when Mitch died, so the hospital called me. I didn't look into his files while I was at the cottage. Just made sure that the place was secure after the ambulance had left. I could meet you there this weekend, and we could look for the will together if that works for you."

"You have access to the cottage?"

"Mitch was a creature of habit. I knew where he hid the spare key, and I felt it was important to protect our son's interests, which is why I went there."

"I could meet you this weekend. When are you thinking of coming up?"

"How about Saturday, say around 11:00? It's number 9 Donovan's Way. Do you know where that is?"

"Yes, I do. I'll see you then." *Well, this ought to be interesting.*

Chapter 2

DONOVAN'S WAY FORKED OFF ROUTE 41 NORTH and continued along the southern shore of Woodson Lake for about a half-mile, ending at Donovan's Cove, where Old Mill Brook emptied into the lake. Gaby parked off the road, just ahead of the gravel driveway leading to 9 Donovan's Way.

Heading down the driveway, Gaby pulled her beanie over her ears and long black hair. The cascade of hair partially screened the scar that ran along her left cheek, a constant reminder of the knife attack that had killed her husband Joe six years ago.

Although it was late April, a brisk breeze blew off the lake, and Gaby was glad she had worn a heavy turtleneck sweater along with a quilted vest. The briefcase hanging from her shoulder was the only indication that this was a business visit.

A late-model silver BMW was parked next to a well-worn Jeep Wrangler in a startling shade of turquoise reminiscent of the Caribbean Sea. A tall woman emerged from the BMW as Gaby approached. She was dressed in black tights, knee-high boots, and one of those bubble jackets that did nothing to flatter her ample figure.

"Mrs. Mitchell?" Gaby asked, extending her hand.

"Attorney Quinn?" she responded, giving Gaby's hand a firm shake. "Thanks for coming. And please, call me Eleanora."

"Most people call me Gaby."

As they walked toward the entrance to the cottage, Eleanora stopped to look out over the lake to the waterfall that gave the town its name.

"I'm always surprised by how beautiful it is here. So peaceful and quiet. Such a contrast to the hustle and bustle of the city. But then, I remember how antsy I got when Mitch and I were up here. Couldn't wait to get back to the pace of city life."

"It's a beautiful setting. These properties along the lake may have once been fishing shacks, but I'm sure they're prime real estate nowadays." As she took in the scene before her, Gaby noted the dock that extended into the lake. Two Adirondack chairs framed a small table, the perfect setting for relaxing with a glass of iced tea on a hot summer day. A bright blue fiberglass rowboat was propped against a birch tree, the oars leaning on the tree beside it.

"Mitch loved to take that rowboat out in the early morning before the lake got busy with visitors."

Eleanora turned toward the house, and Gaby followed.

"Oh, my goodness!" Gaby exclaimed. "Is that an outhouse?" The weathered wood structure with a telltale crescent moon cut into the door was nestled at the edge of a wooded area to the left of the cottage.

"A remnant of long-ago days," Eleanora responded. "We used it to store gardening equipment and such, despite all the spiders and other creepy-crawlies. There's no garage."

"How fun!"

Turning to the cottage door, Eleanora reached up behind the wooden gutter that ran the length of the building and pulled down a key. "Like I said on the phone, Mitch was a creature of habit." She opened the door.

"Ta-da!" She invited Gaby into the cottage, giving her a few moments to take in the layout. The front door led into an open space dominated by a massive stone fireplace.

"I wanted to use an open concept when I designed the renovation of the shack. It had been divided into several tiny rooms. Wood paneled, very dark and dingy. I'm a designer, by the way. I was quite pleased with the way this turned out, though it doesn't look as though Mitch did much to maintain the place."

"It is remarkable, especially with the views of the lake. The cottage is so close to the water, it's almost as if you're standing on a boat," Gaby remarked.

"Exactly the effect I was looking for. I did the design," she repeated. "Rusty Dolan did the work. Do you know him?"

"Yes, actually. He did the renovation of my cottage. He's a fine craftsman."

"Good looking, too. And such a lovely person. He could make a fortune in the city. I talked with him about teaming up, but he said he'd never leave Woodson Falls. I understand his wife isn't well?"

"Maggie was seriously injured in a skiing accident. She's in a wheelchair. Rusty's totally devoted to her." Gaby said. "The fireplace was already in the shack?" she asked, changing the subject. "I bet you could cook in there."

"Exactly. It's huge, and it was the only heat source for the entire shack. Of course, I put in a new HVAC system when we renovated so we didn't need to keep feeding a fire to stay warm on chilly nights. But the fireplace itself is quite stunning."

To the right of the enormous room, French doors led to a sunroom that, at first glance, seemed to Gaby to serve as a collection spot for discarded items. She could see an old desktop computer and printer, boxes of newspapers, and what looked like a rowing machine draped with clothing.

Eleanora had followed the track of Gaby's gaze. "Mitch was fanatical about staying in shape. I think he was over-compensating for his lost leg. You know he lost both a leg and an eye in the war, at the tail end of Vietnam. In any event, if he couldn't get out on the lake, he'd come in here and row his heart out. Oh, sorry… Poor choice of words."

Gaby walked farther into the room, toward the galley kitchen at the other end. "Were you married long?"

"Close to twelve years. We divorced about eight years ago, but the marriage had fallen apart long before then. Stayed together for our son's sake. You do that, then wonder whether it was the right thing. Strong personalities who didn't always see eye-to-eye on things. We were a handsome couple, though. Had a couple of really great years but the next ten, not so good."

"I'm sorry. Didn't mean to intrude."

"That's okay. Water under the bridge. I'm happy where I am, doing what I'm doing. I'll be happier when all this is settled though." Eleanora led Gaby past the galley kitchen and toward a large room. On the way, Gaby spotted a staircase backing the fireplace, a small bedroom that looked as if it had been in use, and a guest bath.

Pointing to the staircase, Eleanora said, "We finished the attic space for Timothy. A bedroom and playroom are up there, plus a bath. Gave him some privacy whenever he was home from boarding school."

And you as well, I imagine.

Coming to the far doorway, Eleanora motioned Gaby into the room. "We added this space as part of the renovation. It was designed as a master suite, complete with a private bath. Mitch used it as his office after we split. If he had a will, this is where it would be."

The large room had a fireplace at the far end opposite the doorway, with built-in bookcases on either side. Wrought iron tools stood at one end of the fireplace; a large basket filled with wood at the other end. A huge picture window faced the lake. Gaby could see a deck just outside that was likely accessed through the kitchen. The wall opposite the window was faced with intricate stonework that mirrored the room's fireplace. A horizontal filing cabinet stood between the door to the room and the one leading to the bathroom. In the middle of the room was an oversized desk. A laptop computer and a simple printer sat on top of the desk, along with a pad of lined paper and a jar of pens and pencils.

"Guess I'll start the search for a will in here," Gaby said, putting her briefcase down beside the desk and heading to the horizontal file. She felt awkward rummaging through Mitchell's papers without having been officially retained as attorney for the estate. Still, it seemed as if Eleanora was trying to protect their son's interests and, as Mitchell's son, Timothy would have a beneficial interest in his father's estate.

"These files are super-organized," Gaby remarked. "Looks as if all the materials related to each of Mr. Mitchell's published books are here. Research, early drafts, correspondence, contracts, reviews, reports of sales and royalties."

Eleanora drifted toward the window, gazing out at the lake as if she would memorize the view. "Mitch was anal about his writing career," she commented. "I don't imagine there's a scrap of paper related to any of those books that Mitch hasn't carefully filed away in its proper place." She paused. "That was one of the problems in our marriage. He was more closely wedded to the French and Indian Wars than to me."

"Are all of these titles still in print?" Gaby asked. "Looks to be about eight of them."

"I believe so, but then I never kept track after we divorced." Eleanora turned from the window. "I need a glass of water. Can I get you anything? Don't know what's in the refrigerator, but I could brew a cup of tea."

"No, thank you. I'm fine."

Gaby turned her attention to the desk. The massive mahogany desk held a large center drawer, with drawers on either side and file drawers beneath. Now that she was next to the desk, Gaby saw it was littered with those stickers found on fresh fruits and vegetables. It looked as if Mitchell favored Gala apples and Bosc pears, although there were a few Granny Smith stickers among the collection on the desk.

Opening the center drawer, Gaby found more pens and pencils, some yellow markers, a ruler, paper clips, Post-It notes in various sizes, a roll of stamps, and several notepads. The right drawer contained a stack of legal pads, and Gaby wondered whether Mitchell drafted in longhand before turning to the computer. The file drawer beneath held what appeared to be research and correspondence related to his current book.

Eleanora returned with a large glass of water, taking up her spot by the window. "Finding anything?"

"Not yet. This drawer seems related entirely to whatever book he was working on."

Gaby turned to the other side of the desk, beginning with the drawer to the left of the center drawer. She was surprised to find a gun that appeared to be fully loaded. Beside the gun were an extra magazine filled with ammunition and a box of .32 caliber bullets labeled "Personal Defense." She recognized the gun as a Beretta from the personal protection course she had taken after recovering physically from the attack that had killed Joe, shattered her ankle, and scarred her face. Although she had qualified for a concealed carry permit in Connecticut, she had never taken the next step and actually purchased a gun.

Quickly shutting the drawer without saying anything about the gun to Eleanora, Gaby opened the file drawer below and searched through the files it held.

"If the will is anywhere, it will be here," Gaby remarked, pulling out a file labeled "Legal."

Chapter 3

GABY MOVED FROM BEHIND THE DESK toward the leather sofa that stood against the stone-faced wall. The wooden coffee table in front of the sofa was stained with condensation rings. She could imagine Mitchell sitting here to go over a draft of the day's work, do some research, or even catnap.

"Maybe we can sit here and review this file together," Gaby called to Eleanora, who was still gazing out the window.

"I'd prefer the kitchen, if you don't mind," she said. "The light is better there."

"No problem." Gaby grabbed her briefcase and followed Eleanora to the counter that formed a sort of breakfast bar between the kitchen and the large room beyond. She nestled into one of the bar seats while Eleanora refilled her water glass, then sat in the other seat after flipping a switch that lit the pendant lamps over the bar.

"Okay. First, there's a copy of the power of attorney." Turning the pages of the document to the end, she said, "It's dated just over a year ago. Looks like Mr. Mitchell named an Alan Waterman as the person to act for him on financial matters. Do you know who he is?"

"Oh, Alan. He's Mitch's literary agent. They've worked together for years. Actually, way back to the first book Mitch published. Really nice person. I like him a lot. Spiffy dresser."

"Of course, Mr. Mitchell's death invalidates the power of attorney. Still, it's important to know who your ex-husband trusted with his financial affairs. Next, looks like a healthcare proxy and living will."

"What are those?"

"They give someone the authority to act on health matters if the principal is unable to make healthcare decisions. Also, the living will expresses the person's end-of-life wishes in terms of the care they would want to receive, or more accurately, *not* want to receive. Looks like Mr. Mitchell gave that power to a Danielle St. Claire. Do you know who she is?"

"I've heard the name," Eleanora responded, getting up and pacing the length of the large living area. "Not sure whether she's a literary assistant. You know, someone who does the footwork for research, proofs drafts, and the like. Or, more likely, she could be one of a string of his many mistresses. At his age, you could hardly call them girlfriends. But if that was drafted over a year ago, he probably had moved on by now. I'm sure I don't know if she's still in the picture."

"Well, again, that power is no longer relevant," Gaby said, setting the document aside. "Aha! Here's a conformed copy of the will."

Eleanora returned to her seat. "Conformed? What does that mean?"

"In Connecticut, the person making the will must sign in the presence of two witnesses. After a will is executed, the drafting attorney often keeps the original will and gives the client a copy—the conformed copy—that indicates when the will was signed and who the witnesses were."

"Does it matter?"

"The court usually is reluctant to accept anything but the original will. The copy is for the client's records, but it isn't valid for the purpose of probate."

"Oh. So how would you find the original, assuming you'd take the case?"

"The original is likely with the drafting attorney. Mr. Mitchell used Thompson & McGill. They have branches all over this part of

Connecticut. The attorney who took the witnesses' signatures most likely is the one who drafted the will. His name is Andrew Stockton. If I was retained by the proposed executor, I'd contact him to request the original."

"Well, of course, Timothy would retain you."

"Let's see who Mr. Mitchell named as executor," Gaby replied, leafing through the document. "He did name your son as executor, as you suspected. He named Alan Waterman as successor executor, in the event Timothy couldn't act in that capacity."

"See! I told you Mitch would name Timothy. What else is in that folder?"

Moving to the next document in the file, Gaby said, "It looks like Mr. Mitchell created a living trust for intellectual property at the same time the will was drafted. The trustee for that is responsible for issues related to copyright, publication and distribution of Mr. Mitchell's intellectual property, in this case, his literary works. Also, the trust would receive and distribute, under its terms, any royalties paid for the works as well as any income generated in speaking fees and the like. It looks like the trust was set up to manage Mr. Mitchell's writing-related income during his lifetime and then following his death."

"Couldn't that be taken care of in the will?"

"It's a complex business. For example, if Netflix or some other streaming service wanted to use Mr. Mitchell's books to create a television series or standalone movies, the right to do so would have to be negotiated with the trustee of the trust rather than with the executor. It's possible your ex-husband wanted his agent to take over the financial aspects of his literary career, perhaps so he could focus more fully on his writing. I imagine that Mr. Mitchell thought dealing with his literary works would be a burden to your son if he was acting as executor. It also would require the estate to remain in administration for a long time, given the number of books Mr. Mitchell published and the likelihood they will continue to be sought after for some time to come."

"That makes sense. I do hope Timothy is a beneficiary of the trust. Mitch's writing was the major source of his income."

"That will depend on the language of the trust, which I'd have to read more closely. In the meantime, it looks like Mr. Mitchell named Alan Waterman as the trustee, which makes sense since you told me he was Mr. Mitchell's literary agent. He would have the knowledge and skills to deal with your ex-husband's works. I'd have to dig further to understand how the trust would work now that Mr. Mitchell has passed away."

"Now then. Since my son has been named executor, I'd like you to represent him."

"I'd be happy to represent him, but the request has to come from him." Gaby took a business card from her briefcase and handed it to Eleanora. "I know Judge Taylor gave you my phone number, but I'd like to give you my business card for reference. Why don't you have your son call me. I'll outline what would be involved if he agreed to serve as executor and give him the option of contacting the drafting attorney in the event he would prefer that attorney to represent the estate."

"Okay, but I really hope he retains you. You know this town, and Judge Taylor *did* recommend you."

"I appreciate that, but it's ultimately Timothy's decision." Gaby picked up her briefcase and extended her hand to Eleanora.

"Why don't you take the file with all those documents in it?" Eleanora said, giving Gaby's hand a perfunctory shake. "I know Timothy will be hiring you, so at least you'd have the file for reference."

Gaby accepted the file reluctantly, recognizing that the strong-willed Eleanora was likely to prevail with her son. "Okay, for now. I can always forward the file to your son if he decides to retain different counsel."

"He won't. Believe me, he won't," Eleanora said as she headed to the cottage door with Gaby trailing behind. After returning the key to the nail behind the gutter, Eleanora turned to Gaby and said,

"Well, lovely to meet you. I'll have Timothy call you this evening if I can reach him tonight. Otherwise, expect a call tomorrow. We'd both want to move ahead with this as quickly as possible."

"I'll expect his call. Thanks for meeting with me today. Have a safe drive back to the city," she said as Eleanora got back in her car, and Gaby made her way on foot up the driveway.

Chapter 4

TIMOTHY MITCHELL CALLED late Sunday afternoon. Gaby outlined the duties of an executor and explained his option to retain his choice of counsel to assist with estate issues, mentioning the attorney who had drafted the will. He was both surprised and pleased that his father had named him as executor and asked Gaby to serve as the attorney for the estate.

"My mother raved about you and said the probate judge had recommended you. Plus, you live in Woodson Falls, which probably will help," he said. "Problem is, my coursework up here at Harvard won't allow me to do much in the way of hands-on work. I'll be able to sign forms and consult with you along the way, but that's about it. Would that work?"

"It should," she replied. "But I think it would be helpful to meet early on so I can get your input on the important issues, especially concerning the house and its contents."

"Mother's Day is next Sunday. I was planning to drive down to New York on Saturday to see Mother before heading back to Harvard to finish up exams. I could stop in Woodson Falls on my way to the city."

"That'd be great. Just let me know when to expect you, and I'll meet you at the cottage. In the meantime, I'll send you a representation letter that outlines the work I'll be doing and my fee, along with some other information. You'll need to sign that and return it to me in order to retain me as attorney for the estate."

"No problem. I'll sign and return it as soon as I get it." Timothy gave Gaby his contact information at the college as well as his cell number and email address. Gaby planned to post the representation letter Tuesday before heading out to breakfast at the café. While it would be good to have the signed copy in hand before meeting with him the following Saturday, she definitely would need the letter before approaching the drafting attorney with a request that he release the original will to her.

With Timothy's verbal confirmation that he would retain Gaby's services as attorney for the estate, Gaby began the work to formally open the estate in the probate court. She wanted to have the paperwork ready for his signature when they met over the weekend. She also reviewed the will and trust documents more carefully so she'd be able to explain each to Timothy, even though she was providing him with copies of both.

Besides naming his son as the executor of his will, Mitchell had bequeathed the cottage to Timothy with the stipulation that Danielle St. Claire had the right to occupy the cottage for a period of eighteen months following Mitchell's death so long as she paid the costs of maintaining it during the time she lived there. This right was exclusive to St. Claire and not transferable to another party. This provision of the will suggested St. Claire was of some significance in Mitchell's life, and Gaby wondered how Timothy felt about this. Did he even know of her existence? If St. Claire was just one in a long string of mistresses as Eleanora had suggested, it was doubtful she would be included in Mitchell's will. And given how fastidious Mitchell was with his records, it was more probable he would have changed his will if the affair had ended badly. There had clearly been a relationship of some importance between Mitchell and St. Claire, whether Eleanora knew of it or not.

This probability was further underscored by an outright bequest to St. Claire of the lesser of $100,000 or twenty-five percent of the remainder of Mitchell's estate, excluding the value of the cottage. Timothy was to receive the rest of what looked to be a substantial estate. These two bequests, however, did not include any interest in Mitchell's intellectual property, which the will indicated was dealt with separately in the Phillip Mitchell Intellectual Property Living Trust.

The trust document was lengthy and complex. Gaby planned to provide Timothy with a written translation of its provisions so he would be able to understand what it dealt with. In essence, all the rights and privileges associated with Mitchell's intellectual property in whatever form, inclusive of any works published prior to his death as well as any additional works in progress at the time of his death, were to be held and invested by the trustee of the trust. During his lifetime, Mitchell received all income in quarterly installments, less expenses of his agent, accountants, taxes and such. All monies that had accumulated but not yet been paid at the time of Mitchell's death were to go to Timothy, free of trust. After that, all earnings from Mitchell's intellectual property, except for expenses, were to be distributed quarterly, with seventy-five percent going to Timothy and twenty-five percent going to St. Claire. As trustee, Alan Waterman was entitled to a reasonable fee for administering the trust in addition to any fees earned as agent for Mitchell's creative works. "Reasonable" was not defined in the document, but Gaby had found that most trustees of active trusts charged about three percent of the total value of the trust as an annual fee.

Although Gaby had not yet delved into Mitchell's finances, it seemed neither Timothy nor his mother would need to worry about the costs of his Harvard education. These should be amply covered by Timothy's inheritance, with more to spare.

Gaby planned to head to Town Hall the next morning after breakfast to get copies of the deed to Mitchell's cottage from the town clerk's files and an estimate of the value of the property at 9 Donovan's Way from the assessor. The tax collector would be able to provide the assessed value of the Jeep she had seen at the cottage as well as any other vehicles owned by Mitchell. All this information was required for the inventory that had to be submitted to the probate court early in the estate administration process. While only a short time had elapsed since Mitchell's death, Gaby hoped his death certificate had arrived in the town clerk's office. Otherwise, she'd need to go to Prescott to pick up the official death certificate to include with the application to open the estate. She'd probably have to head there anyway to collect the original will from Attorney Stockton at the Prescott offices of his law firm, Thompson & McGill.

Gaby sat in a booth at Peggy Huntington's Sunshine Café the next morning, leafing through one of the many gardening books she had picked up from the library. Long-time waitress Helen Wilson came over and poured coffee into Gaby's cup.

"Same breakfast, hon? Two scrambled, bacon, biscuits, no potatoes?"

"Sounds good. Thanks."

"Getting ready for planting?" Helen said looking over at the book Gaby was leafing through. "I can't believe it'll be Mother's Day soon, when most folks around here start their gardens."

"So I've heard. I'm just trying to get acquainted with the different flowers I've seen in my grandparent's garden over the years. I know the difference between annuals and perennials but not much else."

"Good luck with that. I'll be right back with your breakfast," Helen said as she headed to the kitchen for Gaby's order.

A while later, Helen approached with the coffee pot and refilled Gaby's cup while removing her empty breakfast plate.

"Anything else, sweetie?" she asked, plunking down the check.

"No thanks. I'm fine," Gaby replied.

"I was thinking," Helen added. "Nell Whitney might be able to help you with your flower investigation."

"Good thought! I'll stop in there after I'm done in Town Hall. Thanks."

Chapter 5

Nellwyn Whitney was waiting on a customer when Gaby wandered into her shop later that morning. Rainbows & Unicorns offered an eclectic mix of herbs and teas, incense and candles, crystals and semi-precious stones, dream catchers and jewelry as well as assorted stuffed unicorns peeking out from the shelves and hanging from the rainbow-colored ceiling. New Age music played softly in the background as Gaby sank into a comfortable loveseat to wait for her long-time friend to finish up with her customer.

Nell had left a lucrative law practice as a personal injury attorney in New York City, moving to Woodson Falls years ago and opening the small store that attracted visitors from the surrounding area. Her background in the law made her a perfect mentor for a new lawyer like Gaby, who was practicing independently. She used Nell as a sounding board when puzzling over one or another issue she encountered in her practice.

"Gaby!" Nell called, coming over to hug her. "How are you? So good to see you! Anything new on the Jorgenson case up on Lakeview Terrace?"

"Good to see you too, Nell. No, no word yet, but I'll certainly let you know if I learn anything more."

"Good. So, what brings you to town?"

"I had to check some things in Town Hall for a new case and thought it might be a good time to pick your brain about gardening."

"Pick away," Nell replied with a smile, sitting in a rocker next to the loveseat. The diminutive woman was wearing a gauzy caftan festooned in the yellows, purples and whites of crocuses, a perfect reflection of the season.

"I want to restore my grandparents' garden at the cottage, but I just don't know where to begin."

"Has the garden been in bloom since you've been living there?"

"Wildly! Green shoots are popping up, but I'm not sure how to tame what turns into a pretty unattractive jungle by July. I don't want to start pulling out plants I know nothing about and possibly destroy something of value, but it's too much. I take down the dead stalks each fall, and I had someone mulch the garden bed earlier this spring. It'd be nice to try my hand at bringing it back to life, but I'm at a loss as to where to start."

"Since the garden has been blooming year after year, it's most likely your grandparents planted mostly perennials, and hardy ones at that. Over time, a gardener learns what works best in their soil and sunlight conditions—or the plants tell him what they like. You've been living in the cottage for a while now, so whatever is growing in the garden is happy where it is. The biggest problem is that happy perennials tend to spread over time. A particularly vigorous grower can crowd out and even kill a more timid variety!"

"So, what should I do? I'm afraid I might be overwhelmed if I wait until everything's in bloom, but I do want to tame the garden somewhat. I like the English cottage garden look more than the structured gardens I saw in the gardening books I picked up at the library. But I fear what I have is too much of a good thing."

"You're probably right. Even in an English cottage-style garden, plants need room to grow. The best way to approach the problem is down on your hands and knees. You'll notice the difference in the foliage of whatever is popping through. Gradually pull a few sprouts that look the same, toss them into a bucket, and move on. Most weeds can be pulled out more easily than flowers, so that's one way to tell, but if you allow a few similar sprouts to continue to grow, over time they'll let you know whether they're weeds or flowers. You can't hurt anything that can't be replaced down the line."

"Well, it's a start, I guess."

"You'll learn as you go. It's the best way, especially for the cottage look you're interested in." Nell got up and went to one of the bookshelves in the shop. "Here, take this. It's a great guide for getting started," she said, handing Gaby a copy of Patricia Taylor's *Easy Care Perennials*. "It's an older book, but it's perfect for a beginner! It'll help you identify what's there, as well as what else you might want to plant down the line."

"Gee, thanks. I'll bring it back when I'm done."

"No need. I have other copies. Now, tell me about your new case!"

"Did you hear Phillip Mitchell died?"

"Yes! So sad. Emma was a-buzz with the news the other day when I stopped in to Mike's for a salad. Quite famous, too. I just love his books!"

"You've read some of his work?"

"Read them all! Have hard copies in my personal library, each signed by Mitchell himself. He gave talks at the library whenever a new title was released. He was quite prolific! Published a book every two years or so. Sorry to see them end."

"I understand his books are set in the French and Indian Wars, which seems like a pretty narrow niche. I know nothing about that period. Isn't that era just a footnote in the history of North America?"

"Not at all! Those wars were pivotal in creating the United States as the country exists today! And Mitchell had a way of bringing those days alive. Each of the books centers on one historical figure, and you see the wars from that perspective and learn something about the individual. I wonder what he was working on when he died."

"Obviously something, given the size of the file he developed on his current project. Not sure what will happen with that."

"It's so sad, but sometimes works in progress die with their authors, especially such a great writer as Mitchell. I carry paperbacks of the works of all Woodson Falls' writers, although he's the most widely known. Folks like to pick up books by people who live in a place they've visited. Probably should order a few more of Mitchell's. Seems interest in a writer's work increases for a while after they pass away, much like other artists."

"Just how do you know so much about so many things?"

Nell laughed. "Just curious. And I like to delve—to indulge my curiosity! So, is that the case you're working on?"

"Yes. I met with his ex-wife over the weekend, and she talked their son Timothy into retaining me as counsel for the estate. Mitchell named him as the executor of his will. I'll be meeting with the son on Saturday."

Nell got up and headed toward another of her many bookcases. "Here's a copy of Mitchell's first book," she said, handing Gaby the paperback. "You can learn a lot about a person through their writing!"

"Thanks, Nell. I guess I have a busy couple of days ahead of me, between exploring the garden and boning up on Mitchell."

"Enjoy!"

Chapter 6

TRUE TO HIS WORD, Timothy had signed and returned the representation letter engaging Gaby as the attorney for his father's estate. The letter arrived in Friday's mail. Gaby immediately called the law firm, Thompson & McGill, asking to speak with Attorney Andrew Stockton.

"He's left the firm," the receptionist replied.

"Can you tell me where he's working now?" Gaby asked.

"He relocated to Colorado, I'm afraid."

"Then can I speak with his paralegal?"

"Donna left with him. They eloped," the receptionist responded with a chuckle. "Caught everyone here by surprise. No one even knew they were dating!"

"Hmm… Can I speak with whoever took over his caseload?"

"That would be Attorney Legrande. I'll put you through to his line."

"Thank you. Have a nice day."

Legrande picked up after the second ring. "Attorney Michael Legrande, Trusts and Estates. How can I help you?" he announced.

"My name is Gabriella Quinn. I'm an attorney in Woodson Falls and have been retained by the proposed executor of the estate of Phillip Mitchell, who was a client of your firm. Your predecessor, Andrew Stockton, drafted Mitchell's estate planning documents and kept the originals at the firm. I'll need the original will and trust documents to proceed with the administration of the estate."

"I'm afraid I can't release those documents without our client's authorization," Legrande countered.

"Excuse me? Your client is dead and, as I'm sure you're aware, the proposed executor is under no obligation to retain the services of the firm that drafted the decedent's estate plan."

"Sorry. Again, I'm not at liberty to release the documents to you." Legrande clearly didn't want to let go of the matter, or the fee it would generate in billable hours for an attorney who likely was new to the firm and wanted to prove his worth.

"Would you like me to ask Judge Taylor to issue an order to do so?"

"Judge who?"

"Bud Taylor, Judge of Probate for this district," Gaby retorted, astonished that Legrande didn't recognize the name of one of the key people in the area for probate matters.

"Oh, well. That won't be necessary," a flustered Legrande answered. "If you send me a copy of the representation letter signed by your client, I'll have my paralegal locate the documents and mail them to you. Can you give me your address?"

"How about I pick them up at your firm on Monday morning? I'll bring a copy of the representation letter with me so you have it for your files. I have to be in Prescott on another matter." While Gaby didn't need to go to Prescott as she claimed (Mitchell's death certificate had arrived and been filed at the town hall), she didn't want to give Legrande further time to delay the release of Mitchell's estate documents.

"Okay. That'll work, I guess. The documents will be with the receptionist. You can give the representation letter to her. Nice to talk to you," Legrande responded, abruptly ending the call.

Timothy was leaning against a metallic silver Audi 4, gazing out at the lake, when Gaby arrived, briefcase slung over her shoulder and carrying a tote bag. She'd ordered sandwiches and condiments from Mike's Place, along with assorted beverages. College kids were usually hungry, and the long drive down to Woodson Falls from Cambridge had probably sharpened Timothy's appetite. A meal might help to ease their conversation in the direction Gaby needed to go.

"Timothy? Gaby Quinn," she said, extending her hand as she approached the young man. He was medium height, lean and well-built. His sandy hair hung in eyes moist with unshed tears. Dressed in jeans and a grey sweatshirt, he looked like any college kid. "Nice car."

"Hi," he said, shaking Gaby's hand. "It's Tim, please. Good to meet you. Yeah. Dad bought the Audi for me when I graduated prep school. It's embarrassing to have such an expensive ride, but it *is* a bit of a girl-magnet," he said with a shy smile.

"I brought us some lunch. It's gorgeous out. Can we sit over there, while we eat and talk a little?" Gaby asked, pointing to the Adirondack chairs sitting on the dock.

"That'd be great! I'm famished!"

Gaby emptied the tote of its load of food and drinks. "I wasn't sure what you might want. There are ham and cheese, roast beef or turkey, all on hard rolls." She pulled out mustard, salt, pepper and mayo packets as well as bottles of Coke, lemonade and iced tea. She added a large bag of potato chips to the table, then sat down next to Tim. "Dig in."

"This is fantastic. Thanks!" Tim grabbed the ham and cheese and smeared on mustard. "Yum," he said, taking a big bite. "These from Mike's?"

"Of course. Where else?" Gaby took half the turkey sandwich and an iced tea.

"I always loved it here. All this nature, wonderful carefree summers spent mostly with Dad while Mother remained in the city, tied to her business. There was freedom here."

"Same for me. I spent summers here as a kid. My sister and I stayed with our grandparents while our parents traveled doing research. Lots of great memories."

They munched in silence for a while, then Gaby asked, "So, what are you studying? Or haven't you chosen a major yet?"

"Right now, I'm leaning toward public policy, though I'm not sure what I might want to do with it. Dad suggested I dabble a bit before settling on any one course of study. He believed in being well-rounded. Said it's like sampling everything on a buffet table rather than gorging on an oversized helping of your favorite food and possibly missing out on something special. It's working for me, so far."

"Good advice."

"Did you know my dad?"

"I met him once or twice, but never really got to know him."

"He was a great guy. I can't believe he's gone. Everyone liked him. He never played off his fame as a writer. He enjoyed people and getting to know them. I really miss him. It hasn't even been that long since he died." He sipped on his Coke and stared out at the lake. "It feels so strange, being here without him."

"It's hard. Like riding the waves in an ocean. Just try to keep from letting the sadness overwhelm you. Hang onto the good memories instead," Gaby counseled, recognizing she probably should heed her own advice.

"I'll try. I'm just so glad I got to spend last summer with him."

"Oh?"

"You know he wrote novels set in the French and Indian Wars?"

"Yes, though I haven't read any of them."

"Dad would do all this deep research on the character he planned to build the story around. Then he'd take a field trip to the places where that character had been active in one or another aspect of the Wars. He wanted to get a feel for the locations and individuals involved before he sat down to do the actual writing." Tim paused and tore open the bag of chips. "Want half of this roast beef sandwich?" he asked Gaby.

"No thanks. You go ahead. I still have the other half of the turkey sandwich."

"So last summer, he asked if I wanted to tag along while he researched his latest novel. It was a blast, being with him on a road trip like that and sort of getting a better feel for how he went about his writing."

"Where did you go?"

"Up in the Adirondack Mountains, mostly around Lake George. Beautiful country up there."

"I've never been. So, who was the subject of your father's latest book?"

"Sir William Johnson. One of the unsung heroes of the era. He was an immigrant from Ireland who became rich in the fur trade. Johnson had a knack for combining Indian and white power and ended up leading the charge that drove the French from Canada and opened the path to the creation of what became the United States. He was nicknamed 'the Mohawk baronet,' though few people today know anything about him. Dad's working title for the book was 'Warraghiyagey's Council Fire.'" Tim dipped into the bag of potato chips and pulled out a handful.

"Warra-who?"

"Warraghiyagey was Johnson's Mohawk name, given to him when he was adopted by the Mohawk tribe. The Mohawks maintained a fire in the middle of their long houses. It was called a 'council fire' and was the center of government for the five allied Indian nations in the East. They gathered around the fire to make decisions."

"So, what was Warra-who's council fire?"

"Johnson maintained a similar fire near his enormous home in the Mohawk Valley. That fire was considered the capital of the wilderness—its own center of government. It was where Johnson brokered many agreements with the Indian tribes as well as the frontiersmen. Apparently, he was a physically powerful, even overwhelming, presence, which intimidated many of the people who might otherwise have opposed him. Plus, he was smart, even though he had no education."

"So how did Johnson make such a difference in the French and Indian Wars?"

"Johnson didn't have any formal training in warfare, so he adopted his Indian allies' approach to fighting, which proved formidable against the more formal European style of fighting used by both the French and the British. That and his ability to recruit the native population as well as frontiersmen to bolster the British troops led to major victories that pushed the French army back into Canada and eventually back to Europe."

"Sounds like you got a real feel for what your father was working on. Do you know if he got far into the writing? There's a jam-packed file drawer in his desk that your mother said was likely related to his current book."

"I'm not sure how far he got with it. I just hope someone can finish it."

"Maybe that will be you," Gaby offered.

"I'd love to try. It's a great story, but with coursework and all…" Tim's voice trailed off and his eyes filled with tears that he brushed away with the back of his hand.

Gaby stood and gathered up the remnants of their lunch, packing the empty bottles and papers into her tote while giving Tim time to compose himself. "I know this is fresh for you. Have arrangements been made for a memorial service or burial?"

"Mother wants to do something in New York City where she can play the martyred ex-wife among her friends. I think it would be better to have the service up here, where he lived and worked." Tim grabbed the tote, and they headed toward the house. "I'll have to deal with all that when I'm done with exams and back from vacation. I'm planning to take off to Myrtle Beach for a couple of weeks with some friends. Danielle is the person who really should be making these decisions."

Tim paused and shook his head. "Geez! She probably doesn't even know he died!"

Chapter 7

ONCE THEY WERE AT THE COTTAGE DOOR, Tim reached up to the eave and pulled down the key.

"I wonder how many people know where that key is," Gaby said. "Might be a good idea to change the locks to secure the cottage from trespassers. Would that be okay with you?"

"Absolutely," he replied, handing Gaby the key after unlocking the door. "Could I have a copy of the new key when you have it made?"

"Of course. You'll be inheriting the house, which is one of the things I wanted to discuss with you—the provisions your father made for you in his will and a trust he set up to manage his written works."

Entering the house, Gaby pulled a file from her briefcase along with a legal pad and pen. "Let's sit over here," she said, pointing to the breakfast bar where she had reviewed the estate documents with Eleanora.

Once they were settled, she asked, "Before we go through these documents, can you tell me a bit about Danielle? She's mentioned in both the will and the trust. What was her relationship with your dad?"

"Danielle was Dad's girlfriend. She's so sweet, and she made Dad so happy. He told me he wanted to marry her. Was practically asking for my approval." Tim smiled softly, staring into the distance. "I didn't get to see her much, being up at school and all, but when I did... They were just so good together. And she's a fun person. I hadn't seen Dad so relaxed and happy for a long time.

"I really should have thought to call her after Dad died. I was so shocked and at the tail end of a really difficult semester at school, with exams coming up. Mother kept bothering me about how to pay my tuition now that Dad was gone. Danielle's up in Quebec, so she wouldn't have heard anything about my father's death. Mother is still working on the obituary."

"How did they meet?"

"Dad was in Quebec researching one of his books a few years back. Danielle owns a travel agency there. She specializes in tours of historic sites around the city and surrounding area. Dad took one of the tours to some obscure place he wasn't sure he knew how to get to, and they struck up a friendship. He'd see her when he was in the area and, since she was free to travel, especially in the winter months, she began to visit him down here. She loved being at the cottage. She's a real outdoors-type—loves to ski, both downhill and cross-country—which gave Dad the time and space to write while she was visiting. I don't know how I'm going to tell her he's gone, especially..."

"Especially?"

"Danielle came down to Woodson Falls for a short visit while I was with Dad over Christmas break. After she left, Dad said she had told him she was pregnant. He said she wasn't pushing him to marry her or anything. That she was able to raise their child on her own, if that's what he wanted. It was just that..." Gaby waited, giving Tim time to finish his thought. "It's just that she's in her late thirties, more than twenty years younger than Dad, and he was struggling a bit with that. Said he wasn't looking forward to a squally, crawly infant and dirty diapers at this point in his life. He was in his forties when I was born. Said it was tough enough then, but worth it. He worried that he wouldn't live long enough to have a relationship with this child like the one he has... had... with me. Still, he had an open mind about the situation. He was really in love with her."

"How did you feel about your father having another child? Must have been a shock for you."

"It was, a bit. But when I thought about it... I was an only child. And Mother insisted on me being shuffled off to boarding school when I was ten. The first few years at Holderness up in New Hampshire were so hard. When Dad told me about Danielle having a baby, I thought, 'Wow! It'd be really neat to be a big brother. To give that child something I never had.'"

"How lovely! Well, it's clear from his estate plan that your father held both of you in high regard. That can't replace his love for you, I know, but it says a lot about how he felt." Gaby paused, giving Tim time to compose himself.

"Let me go over what's in your father's will and trust," she continued, "including the provisions he made for both you and Danielle. I've made copies of both documents for you and explanations of each article. As executor of your father's estate, it's important that you understand the documents."

After reviewing both the will and trust with Tim and answering his few questions, which centered on the trust and how it complemented the will, Gaby had Tim sign the application to the court to probate the will and accepting the appointment as executor. Then she said, "You don't seem surprised that your father provided for Danielle as well as for you in his will. How do you feel about that?"

Tim shrugged. "Like I said, Dad loved her, and I'm sure he would want her taken care of, especially if she ended up having his child. And I want to be a part of their baby's life, especially now that Dad has passed away. Let the kid know about our father; what a great person he was. I'm totally fine with Danielle being able to occupy the cottage for a year and a half. In fact, that would give me time to figure out whether I want to sell it or keep it for myself. Or maybe Danielle and the baby will want to live here. Who knows?

"Dad was pretty famous, and I know he made a lot of money from his writing. I'm sure there's more than enough money for both

Danielle and me as well as my little brother or sister, at least for now. I know Mother is concerned about the cost of my education, but I'm not. Dad always told me not to worry about money, just worry about getting the most I could from Harvard."

"Did you ever meet your father's literary agent, Alan Waterman? Since he's the trustee of your father's trust, you'll be dealing with him a lot over the coming years. You'll need to establish a working relationship with him."

"I met him a few times, but I don't know him that well. He's been Dad's literary agent for a long time, way back to when Alan placed Dad's first book with a publishing house. He arranges my father's promotional tours and manages the business side of Dad's writing, so I guess it makes sense that Dad made him trustee of the trust for his written work. Mother adores Alan. It's interesting, though. Danielle was wary of him. Thought he was charging Dad too much and really not doing enough to promote his work. I guess I'll see how it works out with him. Don't have much choice, really."

Although the trust document provided a means for the appointment of a new trustee, Gaby thought it was a bit early to discuss that. Instead she asked, "Do you have some time to go through the cottage together? I need you to point out anything you want to take with you now, any valuables that should be put in storage for the time being, and anything you would want me to sell or donate, like your father's clothing. There's no rush with any of that, but it would be a start. It also would be nice to have things tidied up in case Danielle decides to use the cottage during that eighteen-month period we discussed, or if you want to use it for any reason."

"Sounds okay." Tim glanced at his watch. "I don't need to be in New York until after six to have dinner with Mother. And I won't have to stop for lunch along the way, thanks to you."

Leaving the file and materials Gaby had pulled together for Tim, including copies of the will, trust and application to probate, they made their way to the sunroom. As they started to sort through things to discard or store, Tim said, "I don't know if I can do this right now after all."

"That's okay. It can wait."

"I've been having second thoughts about going to Myrtle Beach with my friends after exams are over," he said, turning back to the main room. "Maybe I should be staying here, dealing with this stuff, even though Mother is urging me to get away for a while. What do you think?"

"Everyone handles a loss like this differently. There's no right way and, frankly, for a while, everything feels like the wrong choice."

"Sounds like you've been there."

"I have. It's best to take it one step at a time. You'll figure it out, eventually. I can go through things here and at least organize the cottage a bit if you decide to go to Myrtle Beach. And I can safeguard anything of value that maybe shouldn't be left in the cottage until you're back from your vacation."

Gaby made her way back to the breakfast bar and picked up her briefcase. "I need to locate your father's financial papers so I can begin working on that aspect of the estate. The sooner everything is moved into an estate account, the sooner you'll be able to pay bills, including your school expenses. Any idea where your father might have kept those kinds of papers?"

"He kept that stuff in his office. Most likely his financial records are in the same place you found the will and the trust." As Gaby headed toward the office space, Tim trailed after her, ending up in front of the bookcases, scanning the titles and pulling down books that, from their identical bindings, looked to be a series of journals.

"That's odd," he said, turning to Gaby. "Dad kept a daily journal—one for each year after he began work on his novels. He said it was a writing discipline that allowed him to do a 'brain dump' that somehow helped the creativity to flow. They're all here, except for this year and the year before. I'll look in the bedroom. I know he wrote in his journal first thing in the morning and often just before he went to sleep."

Tim left the office while Gaby looked through the file drawer where she had found the legal papers. He returned several minutes later. "Wonder where they went? I can't find them anywhere and really wanted to take this year's journal with me."

"I'll be in and out of the house," Gaby said, "but I'll keep an eye out for them and call you or send a text when I find them."

"Okay. It's just weird that they aren't here."

"I found your father's address book in the desk. Do you want me to call Danielle and Alan Waterman, or would you rather make those calls?"

"I'll call Danielle. I can't imagine how I'll break this news to her, but I think it's what I should do. I'd appreciate it if you'd call Waterman. I'm not ready for that yet."

"Good. Like I said, one step at a time—just what you're comfortable with."

"I'll try. And I think I will take off with my friends for a few weeks as I planned… as long as it's okay with you. The trip would give me time to sort this out in my head."

"No problem. I'm here when you need me. Just call me with any questions."

Chapter 8

GABY LEFT THE COTTAGE WITH TIM. "Have a safe trip to New York and a good time in Myrtle Beach," she said as he headed toward his car. "Just call me when you're back home. By then, there will probably be more probate forms for you to sign, and I can update you on where we are in the process."

"Sounds good. And thanks for today. I feel like all of this is in good hands."

Waving to Tim as he drove off, Gaby turned back to the cottage. After she located Mitchell's financial records, she wanted to secure the Beretta and ammunition as well as anything else of value in the cottage. But first, she intended to call Rusty Dolan to arrange for the locks to be changed. Once word of Mitchell's death became more widely known, curiosity seekers were likely to come by, possibly looking for some souvenir that might be of value now that the author had died.

As she made her way toward Mitchell's office, she reflected on her meeting with Tim. She had expected him to be a spoiled rich kid whose attendance at an Ivy League school like Harvard just served to make him feel more privileged than other folks. Instead, she had been pleasantly surprised to find Tim to be quiet, thoughtful and willing to listen. His love for his father was painfully apparent and made Gaby wish she had gotten to know Mitchell when he was alive.

She was also intrigued by Tim's reference to Eleanora as "Mother" while he called Mitchell "Dad." She'd always felt a bit sorry for friends growing up who referred to their parents as "Mother" and "Father." The formality of the titles evoked a distant relationship so different from the warm and loving bond she enjoyed with her own parents.

Pulling out her cell phone, she dialed Rusty's number. A woman answered.

"Hello. You've reached the Dolan's. Maggie speaking."

"Hi, Maggie! Gaby Quinn. How are you doing?"

"Loving this weather. I've been cooped up in the house all winter. It's great to be out in the fresh air, especially on such a lovely day. What can we do for you?"

"I was looking for Rusty to do a small job for me."

"I'll put him on." Gaby heard Maggie calling to Rusty to pick up the phone. When he did, she said, "Bye, Gaby. Come by for a cup of tea sometime. I'd love to see you."

"Thanks. I'll do that."

"What can I do for you?" asked Rusty after they had chatted awhile.

"I need the locks changed on a cottage down by the lake. Number nine on Donovan's Way. It was owned by Philip Mitchell, and I'm concerned that curiosity seekers will try to get into the house now that he's passed away. A lot of people may know where he kept the spare key."

"You mean behind the eave above the door? When I did some work for him a few years ago, he told me how to get into the cottage if he wasn't there. I'm probably not the only one. I heard he had died suddenly. Problem is, we're headed to Missouri to visit Maggie's folks for a week. Won't be able to get to the cottage until we're back, probably Monday the sixteenth or the day after."

"No problem. I don't think his death is widely known yet."

"I wouldn't count on that. Why don't you talk to the resident state trooper? What's his name? Matt Thomas? He might be able to cruise past the place now and then. You might also want to alert some of his neighbors, although most of them are probably summer residents and not back full time in Woodson Falls yet. Maybe even post a notice saying that the property is routinely surveilled and trespassers will be prosecuted."

"Good ideas. I'll do that. Could you call me when you're free to do the work?"

"Sure will. At least that place is easier to get to—and get into—than that house up on Lakeview Terrace you had me break into earlier this spring."

"A whole lot easier. Thanks, Rusty. I'll wait for your call."

Rusty's suggestion that she talk to the trooper was a good one. She hadn't seen Matt in town for a while. She hoped he hadn't been transferred. They'd had a few meals together. Met for coffee now and then. Nothing you could call dating, just companionship, which was nice. She enjoyed talking with him. She appreciated that he wasn't pushing for a serious relationship, at least not right now. He seemed to know instinctively that neither of them was ready for anything more yet, since they were both still mourning significant losses. She could ask Matt, or the trooper who was covering for him, to keep an eye on Mitchell's place until the locks could be changed. She also wanted to ask Matt whether Mitchell had a carry permit for the Beretta and if he knew why Mitchell felt the need to have a gun. She hadn't mentioned the Beretta to Tim and wondered if he was aware of why his father had it.

Digging into the file drawer where she had found Mitchell's legal papers, she pulled out several files dealing with his financials. Mitchell had a substantial brokerage account as well as a separate investment account funding a 529 education savings plan containing close to half a million dollars and a retirement account double that size. No wonder he had told Tim not to worry about money, especially the cost of his education. Those funds would support his son through graduate school if he chose to pursue further education after Harvard. Along with a sizable checking account and a few CDs, Mitchell's estate was worth well over three million dollars, not counting the assets in the trust or the cottage, which had been valued at $1,500,000 by the town's assessor.

Most authors made little to nothing on their creative efforts and had to remain employed at a regular job to make ends meet. Those who, like Mitchell, had broken through to become widely known fared much better, both in the royalties they earned and speaking engagements that generated large honoraria. It looked like Tim and Danielle would be in good shape financially for some time to come. The royalties would taper off over time, but there was plenty of money for Tim to get settled into a career and for Danielle to support the child she was carrying.

Gaby looked around the kitchen for a bag or box she could use to carry any valuables. She found a few reusable grocery bags and stowed the gun and ammunition in one after unloading the Beretta. She opened the laptop to save whatever Mitchell had been working on before his sudden death. It was likely his novel-in-progress was in a file on the computer, so it was important to secure that as well as any personal information that might interest an intruder.

She hadn't seen anything of particular value in the sunroom when she and Tim had been in there, nor was there anything of importance in the large living area that should be secured. She made her way to the bedroom when she heard the bedside telephone ring. Reluctant to pick it up, she waited to see if the caller left a message. He did.

"Mitch? Alan here. I've been trying to get you for over a week now. Please call me back when you get this. I've got a few speaking engagements lined up and…"

Gaby picked up the phone, interrupting the speaker. "Mr. Waterman?"

"Yes. Who's this?"

"My name is Gabriella Quinn. I'm an attorney here in Woodson Falls. I'm afraid I have bad news."

Chapter 9

"Bad news? What's going on?" Waterman asked.

"Mr. Mitchell had a heart attack. He died before the EMTs could get him to the hospital."

"Oh, my goodness! I was just with him a few weeks ago. He was at the University of Scranton to give a talk about his upcoming novel. He looked great. Was in top form. I can't believe he died. When did it happen?"

"Just two and a half weeks ago. Thursday the twenty-first. I was planning to call you later today to give you the news," Gaby replied.

"Does Ellie know? Tim?"

"Ellie?"

"Eleanora, Mitch's ex-wife."

"Yes. Actually, she's the one who got me involved with Mr. Mitchell's estate. I met with her right after Mr. Mitchell died. And yes, Tim knows as well. He just left here for New York."

"I don't suppose arrangements have been made yet."

"No, not yet. I think that's still pending."

Waterman switched into business mode. "I'll get in touch with Eleanora and offer to help her with the obituary. There are a dozen or more calls I'll need to make to cancel arrangements for speaking engagements. I had been calling Mitch to discuss those plans." He paused, then added, "What about Danielle?"

"Tim was going to get in touch with her."

"Good, good. And your name again?"

"Gabriella Quinn. Gaby."

"Well, thank you for letting me know. Please reach out if you have any questions about Mitch's affairs. As his literary agent and trustee of his intellectual property trust, I know just about everything. And I'll want to come up at some point to determine how to handle the book he was working on, see where he was with the draft."

"Let me give you my contact information. I have your numbers from Mr. Mitchell's address book."

After he had taken down the information, Waterman said, "What a bombshell! Thanks again for letting me know. I wonder why Ellie didn't call me."

"Sorry to be the bearer of bad news," Gaby said. "I'll be working on the estate while Tim is away for a few weeks. He was named executor and has accepted the position. I'll call you if—or more likely when—I need your input. And as you'll be transitioning Mitchell's trust from payments to him to his named beneficiaries, please let me know if I can assist with that."

"Okay. I'll be in touch. I better get going," Waterman said before ending the call. "Goodbye."

"Bye."

Hanging up the phone, Gaby thought it was odd that Alan asked about Eleanora before either Tim or Danielle, both of whom were more significant people in Mitchell's life. She noticed the red light flashing, probably the start of Waterman's message before Gaby picked up the phone. She pressed the play button and then erased Waterman's initial words. Thinking that there might be other messages that Mitchell hadn't erased, or that had come in after he died, Gaby pressed the arrow that would take her back to earlier recordings.

Working backward, she played the last message on the tape and heard Tim's voice.

"Hi, Dad. I'm planning to drive down to New York to see Mother on Mother's Day and before I take off with the guys after exams are done. I'd like to stop in Woodson Falls for a quick visit on the way. Let me know if you'll be around. I'd love to see you. Bye."

Pressing the back button again, she heard Waterman's voice. "Good morning, Mitch. Alan here. It's short notice, I know, but I'm not going to be able to drive you to Scranton tomorrow as we had planned. There's a new author's launch the following day that I have to attend in upstate New York. I'll meet you at the university and make certain the sponsors of your talk received the packet of biographical information and the synopsis for your next book. I'll collect the honorarium as usual and then be on my way to Syracuse. Sorry. Tell Danielle I'll take a rain check on dinner. See you tomorrow afternoon."

With another press of the back button, she heard a woman's voice tinged with a French accent. "Hi, love. Great to connect with you the other evening, even if only by phone. I know you'll be off to Pennsylvania Friday and staying there overnight, but I'm going to take your advice and come down to the cottage late in the day on Friday and have the rest of the weekend with you once you're back. As I told you when we spoke, I'll be in Saratoga Springs on Friday morning to arrange a tour for later this summer, and it's an easy drive from there to Woodson Falls. It'd be so lovely to be together before the season gets too busy. No need to call me back. I'll just be there to greet you with a hearty boeuf bourguignon. Alan, too, if he wants to stay for dinner. Kisses."

Most likely, Danielle, Gaby thought, pressing the back button one more time. There were no more messages.

The phone was on a side table next to the bed in the first-floor bedroom. The furnishings looked out of place; the bedcovers thrown back. *Wonder if this is where Mitchell died?* She'd need to get a cleaning service in to restore order to the cottage once any valuables had been secured. She knew firsthand how hard it would be for either Tim or Danielle to have to deal with the grim evidence of Mitchell's last moments. It would still be difficult for them to move in the spaces Mitchell once occupied, but at least she could restore order.

Looking around the bedroom, she spotted a dresser opposite the bed. Mitchell's wallet and cell phone were lying on top of the dresser along with a small bowl of change and a simple key chain with multiple keys attached, including the key to the Jeep outside. She gathered those items and added them to the bag containing the Beretta and ammunition.

Gaby placed the bag holding Mitchell's laptop and this second one with the gun and personal items on the breakfast counter, then headed upstairs to what had been Tim's bedroom and playroom. The spaces clearly had been transformed into a bedroom suite, probably used by Mitchell and Danielle when she visited. Women's clothes hung in the closet and occupied two dresser drawers. Assorted women's toiletries were in the bathroom. Bunches of flowers, now wilted, suggested Mitchell had prepared the bedroom to greet her arrival. Nothing in the room was disturbed, so Danielle must have remade the bed before returning to Canada. Or maybe Mitchell had done the work. But why had the flowers been left here, sitting in vases without water?

The former playroom held a comfortable sofa and a large-screen television, as well as a DVD player and elaborate sound system. DVDs filled one shelf of a bookcase, CDs another. Beyond the electronics, which were much too bulky to take with her for safekeeping, there was nothing particularly valuable to be secured in either space, so Gaby returned downstairs and went about drawing the blinds and drapes in the front of the house. The sunroom windows couldn't be shielded from curious eyes. Perhaps the presence of Mitchell's Jeep in the yard would deter snoopers.

With that thought in mind, Gaby dialed the resident state trooper's office, even though she knew Woodson Falls had spotty coverage over the weekends and Matt Thomas was unlikely to be there.

The call was forwarded automatically to the Southbury barracks. She explained her concern about Mitchell's cottage, requesting that whoever was covering the town over the weekend keep an eye on the place. The officer she spoke with said he would convey the message but suggested she also alert neighbors.

Ready to leave the house, Gaby created a sign as Rusty had recommended, securing it to the cottage door with thumbtacks she found in a kitchen drawer. Satisfied she had accomplished all she could, she relocked the door, dropping the key into her pocket rather than replacing it under the eave. She'd meet Rusty here when he was able to change the locks.

The sun was setting as Gaby walked back to her car at the head of the driveway, the sky painted in pink and apricot streaks that were reflected in the lake. She stowed her briefcase and the bags containing Mitchell's valuables in the trunk of her Subaru and made her way to the neighboring properties down the road. The cottages were dark and clearly unoccupied. No cars sat in the driveways. It was weeks before the summer folks would begin to arrive. They usually waited until Memorial Day weekend, which marked the unofficial start of the summer season. At least that might serve to minimize the number of inquisitive people invading Mitchell's property.

Chapter 10

THE PHONE WAS RINGING when Gaby and Kat returned from their morning run. "Law offices, Gabriella Quinn speaking," she announced.

"Hi, Gaby. It's Tim. Tim Mitchell. I'm calling from the airport. Me and my friends are leaving for South Carolina in a few minutes, but I wanted to catch you before we got on the plane."

"Okay."

"I've tried to reach Danielle off and on all this week, but I haven't been able to connect with her by cell or on her home phone. Could you check with her office to see where she is? I don't have that number. Danielle has relatives in Europe, and it's possible she took some time to visit them. The office staff would know where she's at and how to reach her."

"I can do that, Tim. Anything else?"

"Did you come across my father's missing journals while you were going through the house?"

"No, but I'll keep looking. I was able to connect with Alan Waterman, so he's been informed."

"Yeah. He called Mother and is helping with the obituary. We're putting plans for a memorial service on hold until I'm back from the beach. Dad's body was cremated, so there's no rush. I'd still like to have Danielle involved in planning the service." He paused. "She's

49

going to freak out when she hears Dad died, but I can't do anything about that."

"No, you can't. I'll work on things from this end. Enjoy your time with your friends. I'll text you when I contact Danielle's office. And if I come across the journals, I'll hold them in safekeeping until you get back."

"Thanks, Gaby. They're boarding now. Bye. I'll call you when I'm back."

"Bye, Tim."

Gaby filled Kat's water bowl, then went to her office and organized the files on her desk. She tried to keep her weekends free except for occasional meetings with clients, as she had with Eleanora Mitchell and then Tim. Now she was ready to get back to work.

Rummaging through the files she had taken from Mitchell's desk, she found his address book and dialed the number for St. Claire's Quebec office.

"*Bonjour. Ici et La. Pais-je vous aider?*"

"*Parlez-vous anglais?*" Gaby's French lessons had ended with her graduation from high school, and she wasn't about to attempt this conversation in that language. Not only would she have no idea how to ask the questions she had, she knew she wouldn't understand the answers.

"*Oui.* Yes, indeed. How may I help you?"

"Thank you. I'm looking for Danielle St. Claire. Can you connect me with her?"

"What is this regarding?"

"It's a personal matter."

"Mademoiselle St. Claire is not available. Can I connect you with her assistant, Madame Dupont?"

"Yes, thank you."

There was a long pause. Gaby could hear voices murmuring but not what was being said, then, "This is Anna Marie Dupont, Mademoiselle St. Claire's assistant. How may I help you?"

"My name is Gabriella Quinn. I'm an attorney in Connecticut. I'm calling about Ms. St. Claire's friend, Phillip Mitchell."

"Oh, yes. We have met Monsieur Mitchell. They are very close, no?"

"Yes, yes, so I understand. I'm calling with news concerning Mr. Mitchell. Can you tell me how I can reach Ms. St. Claire? Mr. Mitchell's son hasn't been able to contact her and thought she might have gone to Europe to visit relatives there."

"I'm afraid we don't know where she is. She would have told us if she planned to be out of the country, especially this close to the start of the season. Indeed, Mr. Mitchell called here looking for her."

"When was that?"

"Let me see. It was a month ago today. Eighteen April. He said she had planned to drive from Saratoga Springs to his cottage the Friday before and stay the weekend, which we knew, but she wasn't there when he returned from a speaking engagement, despite his finding the ingredients for the dinner she'd planned to make. So, we know she made it to Connecticut safely. We expected her back in the office late that same day, Monday, but she never arrived.

"We did call our contact in Saratoga Springs and learned that Mademoiselle St. Claire had arrived as planned on Friday. She was there at ten in the morning, stayed for lunch, then left at two for the drive to Connecticut. Yet that was the last time anyone seems to have seen her. We asked the RCMP—the Royal Canadian Mounted Police—to see if she might have been in an accident on the way from Connecticut back to Quebec just in case she chose to return early. So far, they haven't learned anything."

"Hmm… She left no messages?"

"No. Nothing. Very unlike Mademoiselle St. Claire. If you locate her, would you please have her call the office?"

"Of course. And would you call me if you hear from her?" Gaby provided her contact information. "Thank you for your help. Oh, one more question. Do you know how Ms. St. Claire planned to get to Saratoga Springs and on to Connecticut?"

"Why, she would drive, of course. She usually drives to visit locations for our tours."

"Do you know what type of car she drives?"

"Of course. It is a Honda Civic Si. Two-door. Bright red. She trades in for a new car every two years; always the Civic Si."

"Thank you so much. You've been very helpful. I'll let you know if I learn anything. Goodbye."

"*Au revoir.*"

What's that all about? Where could she be? Gaby hadn't seen any evidence St. Claire had made it to the cottage on Donovan's Way, but then she hadn't really looked for any. After hearing her message on Mitchell's answering machine, Gaby assumed Danielle had been with Mitchell over the weekend, before he died on the following Thursday. But it sounded as if she might never have arrived. Strange. She'd have to examine things at the cottage more thoroughly to see if she could piece this together.

The ringing of her office phone interrupted her train of thought. "Law offices, Gabriella Quinn speaking."

"Morning Gaby. It's Rusty. I have time later today to meet you at the cottage on Donovan's Way to change the locks. Could you be there around two-thirty or three?"

"Sure. That would be great. I'll be there at two-thirty. Come when you can. I took the key to the cottage with me when I left on Saturday, so I'll let myself in if I arrive before you do."

"Great. See you then."

Perfect. She'd get that done, have a better look around for any sign Danielle had been at the cottage, and start the process of straightening out the place. But first, she wanted to go to Mike's Place for a chat with Emma. If Danielle had made it to Woodson Falls from Saratoga Springs as planned, she probably had stopped at Mike's to get the ingredients for the beef stew she wanted to make for Mitchell. And Emma or Mrs. Browning, Mike's cashier, probably would have seen her. That information would help narrow things down, at least.

Gaby changed from her jogging clothes to something more suitable for a visit to town. Before heading out, she spent some time organizing the files she had pulled from her briefcase so they were ready for her to work on when she returned home.

It was mid-morning when Gaby arrived at Mike's. The lull in the deli business made it the ideal time to grab Emma for a quick conversation. She ordered a coffee and waited for Emma to join her. A few minutes later Emma sat beside Gaby and declared, "You got the Mitchell estate, didn't you! Told you so!"

"Yes, I did. I'm wondering if you could fill in a few blanks for me. When I last saw you, it seemed like you were familiar with Mitchell. Did you ever meet any of his lady friends?"

"Only that lovely woman from Quebec. I think her name is Danielle. Like I told you the other day, Mitchell flirted with every woman he saw, young or old, but there weren't any rumors he dated any of them. It was his wife, Eleanora, who was the cheat. A real barracuda, that one. There was even a rumor that the wife had taken up with Mitchell's agent. Danielle was the only woman I ever saw him with after his divorce. She's considerably younger than Mitchell was, but they made a cute couple. So obviously in love. Why?"

"Had you seen Danielle recently? Before Mitchell died?"

"Hmm… Let me think." Emma paused and took a sip of her soda. "Actually, yes. She was in the store the weekend before he passed away. Said she was buying ingredients for a special stew she was making for Mitchell. I imagine his death has come as a shock to her. She's obviously pregnant. Six or seven months along, I'd guess. How did she take the news?"

"That's the problem. I haven't been able to reach her. Mitchell's son Tim has been calling her on her cell and home phone, and I called her office in Quebec this morning. No one seems to know where she is or how to reach her."

"Weird. Well, I'll keep my ears open and let you know if I hear anything."

"Thanks." Gaby looked at her watch. "I'm meeting Rusty at the cottage around two-thirty. Think I'll have lunch at the café. Can you join me?"

"Would love to, but there's no way. I'll have a whole bunch of folks clamoring for sandwiches in a half hour or so. Catch you another time, okay?"

"No problem. Take care, Emma. And thanks for the information."

Chapter 11

"Hey there. Mind if I join you?"

"Matt! Nice to see you. Of course! Please do. How have you been? I haven't seen you around lately."

Matthew Thomas had served as Woodson Falls' resident state trooper for a few months now. He'd helped Gaby with the Pieter Jorgenson case up on Lakeview Terrace.

"Sorry about that. I should have let you know I was going to be away for a while."

"No problem."

"I had some accumulated time off and wanted to take it before Woodson Falls got busy with the summer residents and visitors. Other folks have told me what you did—to expect a totally different feel of the town during the summer, when the population nearly doubles and the place is swamped with day-trippers."

"You look pretty rested. Where did you go?"

"Visited my parents in upstate New York, then went fishing down in the Florida panhandle with an old friend. It was really relaxing. Once I got back to Connecticut, I figured as long as I was working here in Woodson Falls, I should get an apartment nearby. Found a nice place in Prescott. Also took a cue from you and traded in that gas-guzzling Volkswagen for a Subaru."

"Good for you. I guess that means you'll be continuing on here for a while. I'm glad."

"Me too. And you? Has your phone stopped ringing with requests for legal services after the Jorgenson case?"

"I think it's starting to slow down. Hard to tell, there have been so many calls. And I'm doing well. I've been keeping busy with my law cases and trying to resurrect my grandparents' garden at the cottage."

"Let me know if I can help with the garden. I know next to nothing about plants, but I'm good for grunt work."

Gaby laughed. "I'll keep that in mind."

"Anything new on the legal front?"

"One of Woodson Falls' luminaries passed away, and I'm handling the estate."

"Interesting?"

"Pretty much run-of-the-mill, but you could help me with a couple of things."

"Shoot. You know me… Happy to serve," he said with a smile. "I've missed you, Gaby. Thought a lot about you while I was gone."

Helen brought over Gaby's lunch and filled her water glass. "What can I get you, officer?"

"Just one of your breakfast sandwiches, please. And coffee when you have the chance. Thanks."

"Be right out."

Gaby smiled. "Breakfast sandwich? It's lunchtime, or didn't you notice?"

"I got into the office early to see what went on while I was away and was called to a domestic dispute before I could sit down. Never even had time for coffee, and I'm starving. So, what do you need from me?"

"It's Phillip Mitchell who died. The writer."

"Did he live on Donovan's Way? I saw the request that we monitor the place."

"Yes. I requested it since Mitchell was pretty famous, and his house might attract snoopers looking for a souvenir. Anyway, I found a

Beretta in his desk and wondered if he had a carry permit for it and if there might be something in his past that made him feel he needed personal protection. I secured the gun as well as other valuables I found in the house."

"Smart! I can look into that for you. Was there anything about his death that was suspicious?"

"No. It was a heart attack, and he'd had two in the past, so his heart was pretty damaged." Gaby paused. "By the way, I missed you too."

Matt smiled. "Anything else?"

"I was wondering—" The insistent tone of Matt's beeper interrupted her.

He listened to the operator, then got up from the booth. "Sorry, Gab. Gotta run. Bad accident on 41 North."

Helen approached with his meal in one hand, coffee pot in the other. "Sorry, Helen. Duty calls. Can you have that wrapped for me? I'll pick it up when I get back to the office."

"We'll make you a new one."

"Thanks."

"Catch you later, Matt," Gaby called.

"I'll call you," he said as he left the café.

Gaby mused on her slowly evolving relationship with Matt while she ate her lunch. She was attracted to him and knew it was more than his rugged good looks, piercing blue eyes, and dark brown hair touched with grey. More than his lean build, despite what appeared to Gaby to be a steady diet of restaurant food laden with fat. Good looks aside, she felt comfortable with him. She wondered when she'd finally be ready to tell him about Joe and the attack that had killed him and changed her life completely as well as breaking her heart.

Gaby was unlocking the cottage door at 9 Donovan's Way when she saw Rusty's truck headed down the gravel driveway.

"Hi there. Thanks so much for finding time to do this. I just got here. How was your trip to Missouri?"

"Hi yourself. Good. Travel's a bit rough for Maggie, but she's a trooper and was so happy to see her folks. By the way, I stopped at the hardware store to pick up two locksets. I remembered there were only the front door and the door leading to the deck. I see you posted the notice like I suggested."

"It was a good idea. Also called the barracks to ask them to have the trooper covering Woodson Falls swing by the place occasionally."

"Well, let me get to it. Maggie gave me a shopping list a yard long to restock the refrigerator and pantry after being away."

"Thanks. I'm going to straighten up the place a bit in case Mitchell's son or girlfriend wants to stay here."

"Do you know Karen Browning? Works at the post office?"

"Yes, but I haven't seen much of her since the court began requiring documents to be electronically filed rather than mailed. One more nail in the coffin of the U.S. Postal Service, I fear."

"You might want to call her to give the place a good cleaning. She does a nice job as long as you don't mind her coming at odd hours when she's not working at the post office."

"Great idea. That would work. I'll call her."

While Rusty worked on the front door, Gaby made her way to the kitchen. If Emma was right and St. Claire had been in Woodson Falls as planned, the ingredients for the beef stew she was planning to make would be in the refrigerator; maybe even the completed dish, ready to reheat when Mitchell returned from Pennsylvania.

Scanning the kitchen counters for any evidence of cooking, Gaby spied a bottle of quality burgundy standing next to the refrigerator along with a basket holding a head of garlic, some shallots and a dozen or more pearl onions. The refrigerator was minimally stocked, and Gaby suspected Mitchell ate many of his meals at restaurants or, possibly, at the homes of fans in the area. On the top shelf was a package labeled "beef chuck" along with some carrots, mushrooms and new potatoes. A cook herself, Gaby recognized the collection as ingredients for the French-style beef stew called boeuf bourguignon.

Hmm... The assorted stew ingredients suggested St. Claire had been at the cottage, most likely Friday evening as she had planned. But something must have come up that caused her to leave suddenly. Yet no one had been able to reach her, which seemed strange.

Gaby had seen no other evidence of the woman's presence. Her car would have been parked outside if she had taken a walk, had an accident, and was lying in the woods—most likely dead from exposure now, a month later. And she would have brought some sort of luggage as well, if only an overnight bag. It was a mystery where she was. She would be sure to ask Matt to attempt to track down the missing St. Claire. Perhaps check with Prescott Memorial to see if she had been admitted due to some problem with her pregnancy.

In the meantime, she decided to hunt more thoroughly for the missing journals Tim had asked her to find. Starting in the bedroom on the first floor, where it appeared Mitchell had died, she went through the nightstand, pulled back the bed linens, and looked underneath. There was nothing but dust. She turned next to the sofa in front of the massive fireplace in the main room, looking under the magazines on the coffee table and lifting the cushions to see if the journals had somehow slipped down there. No luck.

As she made her way to the office, where she planned to search the sofa opposite Mitchell's desk, Rusty called out to her from the kitchen.

"Don't know if you noticed, but this door to the deck was left unlocked."

"I never thought to try it," she responded. "My bad. I should have checked that before I left the other day. I'll make sure it stays locked as long as the place remains unoccupied. Thanks for the heads-up."

"No problem. I'll swap out this lockset and then be out of your hair."

Once in the office, Gaby checked the bookcase where the other journals were lined up, thinking the missing ones might have fallen behind the others. Pulling down all the books on that shelf, though, she found nothing and went about restoring the volumes to their original locations.

She was kneeling to look under the leather sofa when Rusty came into the room. "Here are the keys to both doors. Like with the Lakeview Terrace property, I'll keep a spare key in case you need me to come here when you aren't available. I'll bill you for the work and the locksets. Take care. I'm off to tackle Maggie's shopping list."

"Thanks again, Rusty."

After he left the cottage, Gaby moved the coffee table aside and felt under the sofa. All she found was dust, reminding her to call Karen Browning. Getting up, she made one last attempt to locate the journals, taking the cushions from the leather sofa and piling them on the coffee table. Hidden underneath where the cushions had been was a cell phone.

Chapter 12

GABY HAD ALREADY SECURED THE CELL PHONE she had found in Mitchell's downstairs bedroom on her last visit, which she assumed was his. The cell phone that had slipped beneath the cushions of the sofa in Mitchell's office could be an old one the writer thought he had lost, but it was a newer model iPhone in a case with a floral design and more likely belonged to the missing Danielle St. Claire. The only way to determine that would be to recharge the phone once she returned home, but Gaby feared the phone's battery might not take a charge since it was fully discharged. It was worth the effort to at least try to revive the phone, though, so she could determine whether it belonged to St. Claire.

Heading home from Mitchell's place on Donovan's Way, Gaby stopped at Frank's Supply Depot to have additional keys to the cottage made. She wanted one for Tim, but also a spare for Karen to use when she cleaned the place, as well as a backup for St. Claire when she finally was located.

Once home, she let Kat out, taking time to play fetch with the dog, which had been cooped up in the house most of the day. It was past seven o'clock and getting dark when Gaby finally plugged in the newly discovered cell phone. Although it was a newer model than Gaby's iPhone, it began to charge as soon as she plugged in her adapter. The phone started pinging a few minutes later, and Gaby left it to continue its recovery, planning to look at it after dinner to see whether any messages, texts or records of missed calls would point to the phone's owner and, if it belonged to Danielle, reveal where she had gone.

She hadn't yet heard from Matt, but hesitated to call him to ask that he initiate a search for the missing St. Claire. This being his first day back in the office after a few weeks away, she knew he was likely swamped with work, especially with the accident he had rushed away to attend to. She trusted he would call her when he could.

It was close to ten when she finally heard from him. He sounded weary. "Hi, Gaby. Sorry it took so long for me to get back to you. It's been one hell of a day."

"Anybody hurt in that accident you were called to?"

"Four people taken to the hospital, two with serious injuries. The person who caused the accident got off without a scratch. Thank goodness the folks who were in the car that was hit were wearing seatbelts. The car itself is a total loss. Anyway, what are you up to?"

"I was trying to figure out if I could get into this phone I found at 9 Donovan's Way. It had slipped between the cushions of a sofa in Mitchell's office and turned up when I was looking for a journal Mitchell kept that his son Tim had asked me to find. I'm hoping it might belong to Danielle St. Claire, but can't tell for sure yet since it's locked."

"Is it an iPhone? If so, you can check the emergency medical ID information."

"How would I do that?"

"Swipe up to access the screen to enter a passcode. Tap on 'Emergency' in the lower left corner, then 'Medical ID' in the same place on the next screen. If the phone's owner has set up their medical information and emergency contacts, you'll be able to see their name and other information there."

"It worked! And, yes, it is Danielle's phone. I can't imagine she'd leave it behind intentionally."

"Neither can I... By the way, you were starting to ask me something when I was called away to that accident." He paused, then asked, "What did you need from me?"

"It'll hold. Why don't you head home and get some rest? We can talk tomorrow."

"If that's okay, that's what I'll do."

"No problem. Sleep well. Tomorrow is another day. Bye, Matt."

"Bye, Gaby."

She smiled as she hung up the phone, happy that he'd remembered to call as he'd promised, even through his obvious fatigue.

Picking up the fully charged phone, she noticed that there were voicemail notifications on the lock screen from both Tim and Mitchell. This definitely was St. Claire's phone. The discovery added to Gaby's concern about just where the woman might be. If she had left the cottage in a rush, she would have been sure to take her phone. Now she hoped Matt would be able to work with Canada's RCMP to find her and said a small prayer that she was safe.

Gaby settled into her office the next morning, working on the draft of an estate plan for a new client. Over time, she had developed an approach to drafting a will that followed the steps in the estate administration process, but she always found it necessary to modify one or more sections to fit a client's circumstances. The ringing of her office phone interrupted her thoughts. She hoped it was Matt.

"Law offices, Gabriella Quinn speaking."

"Good morning, Gaby." She recognized the gravelly voice of her long-time client, Winston Pinkham.

"Good morning, Mr. Pinkham. How are you?"

"Still alive, though I'm not sure how much longer I'll go on," he responded. Having predicted his impending death several years ago, most people tended to smile at Pinkham's consistent pronouncement.

"I'm sure you have a few more days left," Gaby said, "if not weeks or even months. What can I do for you?"

"Bill Harrison asked me to call. He wants me to give you permission to talk with him about this subdivision I'm doing, which is fine with me."

In contrast with his prediction of his imminent demise, Pinkham worried constantly about outliving his considerable wealth. To that end, he had decided to subdivide the property abutting his house, land he had previously earmarked for donation to Woodson Falls' land trust upon his death. He had hired Bill Harrison, an expert in land use law, to assist in the subdivision process, which involved multiple hearings at the town's various land use commissions.

"What is Bill concerned about?"

"I hired an engineering firm to plan the subdivision. They came highly recommended by an old friend of mine. Bill oversees the legal aspects, including adherence to the town's planning and zoning regulations. The land has a brook running through it, so the wetlands regulations are involved as well. All very technical. I think Bill is concerned the engineering firm is taking advantage of me, assuming I'm a doddering fool. I told him not to worry himself, but he wanted to talk to you about it since you hold my power of attorney and will be the executor of my estate when I finally die."

"Well, Bill is the best in his field. He's got a lot of experience in land use, so I wouldn't dismiss his concerns out of hand. I'd be happy to talk to him about this and let you know what he's thinking."

"Thanks, Gaby. I trust you more than anyone else, so I'm glad he wanted to get you involved and that you're willing to do this. I'll give Bill a call to let him know he can get in touch with you."

"That's fine. I'll call you after I've had the chance to talk with Bill."

"Thanks again," he said, hanging up.

Bill Harrison—who looked a bit like an out-of-place surfer, tall with a mop of dark blond hair and a perpetual tan—was a nationally renowned land use attorney who practiced in Prescott but consulted across the country. Gaby had declined his several invitations to accompany him to one or another social engagement. She suspected Bill's life revolved around his law practice, and Gaby wanted more from a relationship, more like the life she had shared with Joe before he was killed.

She turned back to her work but was interrupted by yet another phone call.

"Law offices…"

"It's Matt, Gaby. Sorry about yesterday. What a crazy day! I checked into the question you asked me about Phillip Mitchell's gun permit. He did have a concealed carry permit here in Connecticut. He qualified several years ago and kept the permit current. There was nothing in the records I was able to access to suggest he had any specific reason for having a firearm. He might have just felt a bit vulnerable isolated in the cottage on the lake, especially during the dead of winter. I understand he was divorced and living alone?"

"Yes, he divorced several years ago. Plus, he was a Vietnam War vet, a wounded vet at that. Maybe that made him jittery, and he got the gun as a way to deal with it." *And I got a dog,* she added to herself. "Thanks for looking into that for me amid everything else you were involved with yesterday. It could have waited."

"I know, but I like to stay on top of things as they come up. Good way to declutter the mind," he said with a laugh. "What was the other question you had?"

"Mitchell had a lady friend by the name of Danielle St. Claire. She owns a travel agency called Ici et La, up in Quebec. According to Mitchell's son Tim, Mitchell and St. Claire were very close. She was pregnant by him, and he had planned to ask her to marry him."

"Okay…"

"The weekend before his heart attack killed him, Mitchell was in Scranton, Pennsylvania, to give a talk about his upcoming book. There's evidence St. Claire was planning to come to Woodson Falls the Friday he was speaking, so they could have the rest of the weekend together. Emma over at Mike's Place remembers seeing her that afternoon when she bought ingredients for a beef stew she planned to make for Mitchell. Tim wanted to be the one to tell St. Claire that his father had passed away, but he couldn't reach her. I tried her office. Her assistant knew she had planned to be in Woodson Falls that weekend, but they haven't heard from her and have no idea where she is now. I found the ingredients for the dish she was intending to cook for Mitchell at the Donovan's Way cottage, but there's no car or luggage."

"And?"

"Her assistant up in Quebec thinks she may have had a car accident on the way to Woodson Falls from Saratoga Springs, where she had stopped to make arrangements for a tour, or on her way back to Quebec from Woodson Falls. They did confirm her arrival in Saratoga Springs as planned, and then her departure around two in the afternoon. They've asked the RCMP to look into that, and I was hoping you could connect with them from this end and locate her. She drives a late-model Honda Civic Si, red."

"Plate number?"

"Never asked. Sorry about that. I'm concerned. It's several weeks since Mitchell died, and it appears St. Claire went missing just before then. She's a beneficiary of his estate, so it's important I locate her. And..."

"What else?"

"It still bothers me that I found her cell phone. I doubt St. Claire would have left without it, even if she was in a hurry."

Chapter 13

"Well, aren't you the clever little sleuth, Ms. Gaby," Matt teased. "That's a great bit of investigative work you've accomplished! Of course, I'll reach out to the Canadian authorities to see if together we can track down Ms. St. Claire."

"Thanks, Matt. I don't know why I feel so worried, but I do."

"It's that amazing intuition you've developed. Impossible to ignore it," he responded. "Can you give me the phone number for St. Claire's business up in Quebec? They may have her plate number, and I want to check with them first to see if she's shown up since you spoke with them."

Gaby gave him the Quebec number, then told him she planned to work from home today, but if she was out, he could reach her on her cell if he came up with anything.

"Thanks for taking this on for me, Matt," she said, reluctant to hang up.

"No problem, Gaby. I'll get back to you once I've had a chance to connect with the travel agency and the Canadian authorities."

Sitting back in her chair, she considered what she should tell Tim. She didn't want to alarm him about the missing St. Claire, but she did want to alert him to the fact she hadn't yet been able to contact the woman and also to let him know she had gone ahead and changed the locks to the cottage as planned. She settled on sending him a text message saying she hoped he was enjoying his trip and that work for his father's estate was being handled on this end. She'd fill him in on the details when he returned and arrange to get the new cottage key to him. By that time, St. Claire might even have turned up. No need to worry the young man about something she wasn't sure of yet.

The phone rang again. "Law offices, Gabriella Quinn speaking."

"Gabriella Quinn—just the person I was trying to reach. Bill Harrison here."

"Hi, Bill. I assume Mr. Pinkham called you?"

"Old Pinky. I'm worried the crew he's got involved with that subdivision of his is taking him to the cleaners. I was hoping you could talk some sense into him since I haven't been able to get through, despite my best efforts."

"You call him Pinky?"

"Well, not to his face."

"That's a relief! What's going on?"

"It's pretty complicated. Any chance you'd have time for lunch this week?"

"I'm free tomorrow, maybe Thursday."

"Tomorrow would work. Can I pick you up around quarter to twelve?"

"I could meet you somewhere."

"The place I'm thinking about is out of town. I want to be away from potential eavesdroppers."

"Okay. My place is a bit out of the way. Why don't I meet you at Town Hall?"

"I'll see you there tomorrow then. Bye, Gaby."

Wonder what that's all about.

Next on her to-do list was a call to Karen Browning.

"Hello?"

"Karen? It's Gaby Quinn. Rusty Dolan suggested I call you. He said you were doing some housecleaning, and I wondered if you'd be available to help with tidying up Phillip Mitchell's place on Donovan's Way."

"I heard he passed away suddenly. What do you need?"

"I'd like to have some basic cleaning done so Mitchell's son or girlfriend can use the place if they decide to stay there."

"That would be fine. I'm looking for a little extra work on the side. Problem is, I'm working extra hours here at the post office this week, covering for Sue Harrison, who's on vacation. I hate to blow this opportunity, but I won't be able to get there until a week from tomorrow. That would be next Wednesday afternoon."

"No problem. There's no real rush. Would three that day work for you?"

"Perfect. Where on Donovan's Way?"

"Number nine. See you then. And thanks," Gaby added, hanging up the phone.

That settled, Gaby began work on the probate court's Form PC-440 detailing the property comprising Mitchell's estate. Once that was done, she would mail it to Tim for his signature, then file the signed form electronically with the court ahead of its due date. All the materials she needed for the inventory had been in the files she had found in Mitchell's desk.

The following day was bright but windy. Gaby waited outside Town Hall for Bill Harrison's arrival, tucking herself into his jet-black Porsche convertible before he could leave his seat to open her door. She was happy the weather kept the car's top up and her hair from flying in every direction.

They drove across the border into New York State, the scenery much the same as in rural Connecticut. After half an hour, they arrived at the quaint Cobblestone Inn, rumored to have been a stop on a long-abandoned stagecoach route. There were a few rooms for rent upstairs, but the main floor, built entirely of stone, had been transformed into a restaurant serving lunch most weekdays and dinner on weekends. A fire blazed in the central fireplace, quickly warming them as they took their seats a short distance away.

Gaby had been to the place a few times. The Inn was famous for its oversized drinks, perhaps a way to encourage people to spend the night rather than hazard the roads after a couple of giant cocktails before dinner, as well as a complimentary after-dinner drink on top of generous servings of wine. Equally well-known for its huge popovers served with every meal instead of the usual basket of assorted rolls, the restaurant's cuisine was above average, right down to its standard: turkey hash. Gaby ordered the roast chicken special with rice pilaf and a glass of chardonnay; Bill ordered the rib eye and roasted new potatoes along with a glass of a hearty burgundy.

As they each nibbled on a warm popover slathered with butter, Bill began to explain his concerns about Pinkham's advisors.

"How well do you know Pinkham? He told me he's granted you power of attorney over his affairs as well as named you as executor of his estate when he passes away—a promise he keeps failing to keep," Bill said with a smile. "He obviously trusts you."

"I've been working with him for several years—since I started my law practice, actually. He's a lonely guy, and something is keeping him from engaging with the public at this point in his life, although he was active in the past, particularly in conservation and land preservation issues. Never married. Few relatives. I try to stop in to see him each week. See how he's doing. Bring him baked goodies, which he seems to appreciate. Sometimes he'll call me to discuss some small change to his will, and we'll visit awhile. Then he'll tell me to forget about it as I'm leaving."

"How do you bill for that kind of thing?"

"I don't, unless there's actual work to be done. I've found that elderly folks up here often feel isolated. A visit now and then keeps them engaged with life. Call it charity—or whatever you like. I enjoy older people, especially when you can get them to talk about their early lives in Woodson Falls."

"Are you at all familiar with the piece of property he's looking to develop?"

"Only in passing. He had been planning to donate the property to the land trust upon his death, but like many older people, he's afraid of running out of money. At the same time, he told me he plans to sell two of the lots at a steep discount to friends he claims are helping him with the subdivision. I'm sure that's further complicating the situation."

"You can say that again. It's a difficult piece of property. The terrain is steep, there's a brook running through the middle of the land, which raises wetlands issues, and there's a significant amount of ledge. Still, the percs and deeps that were done early on demonstrate the land can sustain a six-lot subdivision with respect to well and septic installations within the restrictions imposed by the town's health code. That's usually sufficient to guide a developer in mapping out a reasonable subdivision plan, including the percentage of land that has to be dedicated as open space."

"So, what's the problem?"

"It's almost as if these guys are looking for ways to invite the planning and zoning commission to object to one or another aspect of the plan. It's not rocket science, especially for an engineering firm with the expertise this one is noted for. I'm concerned they're running up bills unnecessarily. This should have been approved months ago, yet they keep fiddling with the plan, despite the guidance I offer to keep the lots within the town's subdivision and zoning as well as wetlands and health regulations. I'm at the point where I'm not billing Pinkham for all the hours I'm putting in on this, but it has to come to an end sometime.

"It's going to be expensive enough to construct the road necessary to serve every lot once they're developed. There was a recent change in the town's road ordinance that demands stricter construction standards than in the past. Good for the homeowners and for the town if the road is accepted into the town's road system. But it does create a significant increase in costs to the developer.

"I haven't been able to get these guys to do the appropriate planning for any of it. They seem to be begging for a request for modifications every time they appear before one or another of the commissions involved with the approval process."

"I'm sure you've talked with Mr. Pinkham about your concerns."

"Of course. I've explained to him what's going on and the impact it's having on development costs."

"Does he realize how much that may eat into the price he'll be able to realize once the lots are finally approved?"

"I'm sure he does. I've outlined the maximum anticipated price he can ask for each of the lots and the costs associated with developing them. But it's like he has a blind spot where the engineering firm—as well as his supposed 'friends'—are concerned. I'm not sure what to do, but it feels like a case of elder abuse to me. Isn't there some kind of protection available in a situation like his?"

"Yes, and no. Based on what you've told me, it would be easy enough to demonstrate the firm is taking advantage of Mr. Pinkham. The problem is with Pinkham himself."

"How so?"

"Even moving toward ninety, he has all his faculties. It'd be hard to prove just how he's being duped, especially since so far he's been refusing to consider any evidence to the contrary. How about I talk with him about this? Find out what's behind his reluctance to accept your advice and require this firm to move ahead with the project or resign."

"That would be great. I know he admires you," Bill said with a smile, "as do I."

"So, what else is going on in your life?" Gaby asked. She didn't want to encourage Bill's obvious invitation to develop a closer

relationship. As soon as he began discussing the many consulta-
tions he had scheduled over the next several weeks, she knew she was
making the right decision.

Chapter 14

AFTER THEIR PLATES HAD BEEN CLEARED, Gaby asked for an herbal tea while Bill ordered a hot fudge sundae served over a brownie.

"I know you love chocolate," he said after they had been served, handing her one of the two spoons the waitress had left with the dessert and gesturing to Gaby to take a sample.

"Hard to resist. Why do you always seem to tempt me with one or another chocolate treat?"

"No other way to get your attention," he answered with a smile. "So how do you think we should approach the issues with Pinky's subdivision? At this rate, I'm concerned it will never be approved."

"And I'd be stuck with tackling it as executor of his estate. No, thank you. I'll give Mr. Pinkham a call when I get back to the office. Let him know we've met and talked. But I'd like to see what's going on for myself. Not that I don't trust your assessment of the situation, but Pinkham's already heard—and rejected—your observations and concerns."

"That's true."

"I'd confront the engineering firm or his friends—or both—based on what you've told me, but I'd be on shaky ground. Pinkham's as competent as you or me. It would be fair for either the firm or the friends to ask why I wasn't handling this for Pinkham as his agent under the power of attorney if I had concerns about financial abuse."

Gaby paused to take another spoonful of the sundae. "I'm thinking it might be best if I tell Pinkham what I have observed myself and then, hopefully, guide him toward a confrontation with the engineering firm. They're the controlling element here, not the friends. When's the next planning and zoning meeting? Is Pinkham's subdivision, Sunrise Hills, on the agenda?"

"Yes, but barely. The engineering firm submits the modified application just under the wire, so the matter ends up close to the end of the agenda for each meeting, even now, when the subdivision application is dealt with as old business. That means the firm's principals sit there, tallying billable hours, while the commission deals with items that are earlier on the agenda. I can understand it happening once or twice, but it seems to be a consistent pattern. Along with the small changes they make that end up creating more issues, the matter goes on and on. The meeting is next Tuesday evening. Starts at seven."

"Just what role are Pinkham's friends playing in all of this?"

"They show up at every meeting and argue for modifications to the plans that seem to me to be geared toward enhancing the lots they've claimed for themselves. And the engineering firm plays along because the so-called friends' suggestions just add to the delays."

"What does Pinkham think they're doing for him?"

"Watching out for his interests. But they're doing anything but."

It was too late to go into Town Hall when Harrison dropped her off after lunch. She wanted to review the current plans for the Sunrise Hills subdivision before Tuesday evening so she'd have an idea of what was being discussed at the meeting. She didn't have a complete knowledge of the town's subdivision regulations, but looking at the plans would give her a good sense of the issues, which would be enough to evaluate what was taking place that had led to Harrison's concerns.

Perhaps Miriam Henderson, the town's land use clerk, could help her decipher the latest subdivision plan in relation to the regulations.

Gaby gave Pinkham a call as soon as she returned to her office. She explained she had met with Harrison and understood what was troubling the lawyer but wanted to see for herself just what was going on and whether Pinkham should be concerned.

"The next planning and zoning meeting is this coming Tuesday evening. Why don't I go to that and get a feel for what's happening? Then we can discuss what I've seen and take it from there. I have no reason to doubt that Harrison has a basis for his concerns and is just trying to protect you, but I'd rather judge for myself."

"That would be so good. You know I trust you more than anyone else. I'd value your input on this. Art Fuller, the fellow who recommended Blackberry Hill Engineering to me, is an old friend of mine. I'm confident he wouldn't steer me wrong on this. The firm apparently has a long history of success specializing in land development here in Connecticut."

"Do you think you'd like to come with me? I trust your opinion as much or more than my own."

"No, no. I don't think I'd hold up too well at that kind of meeting. But thanks for the 'atta boy,'" he responded with a chuckle.

"Well, okay. So, we have a plan. I'll attend the meeting next Tuesday evening and report back to you on Wednesday. Do you have anything scheduled that day?"

"No. Nothing going on. Hopefully, I'll still be alive then."

"Oh, Mr. Pinkham, I'm sure you will be," Gaby answered. "I'll see you then. Would ten o'clock work for you?"

"That would be fine. Goodbye now, Gaby. And thanks. You be sure to bill me for your time, both today with Bill and at the meeting. Promise me?"

"Okay," Gaby said reluctantly, knowing Pinkham would write a check to her whether or not she billed him. "Goodbye. Call me if you have any thoughts before Tuesday evening."

That taken care of, Gaby returned to the will she was drafting before ending her workday, planning to review it in the morning.

The phone was ringing the next day when Gaby and Kat returned from their early run. "Law offices, Gabriella…"

"It's Nell, Gaby. Good morning! Lovely day today!"

"Sure is. Just got in from a run. Summer's on the way."

"I have a favor to ask."

"Anything, Nell. You know that. Is everything okay?"

Nell sighed on the other end of the phone. "This one's hard. Any chance of meeting somewhere private so I can explain?"

"Of course. Why don't you come over here? I'm free today—or anytime. It's out of the way, and we won't be interrupted like at the store. Plus, you can take a look at the garden. Tell me if I'm heading in the right direction. I've been following your advice and working on it piecemeal each weekend."

"I'm tied up with the store today and tomorrow as well as on Sunday. Would Monday work? The store is closed then. Are you free anytime that day?"

"Nothing on the calendar. Why don't you come over for a light lunch?"

"That would be great! See you about 11:30, 12:00?"

"Whenever. I'll be here."

"Thanks so much, Gaby. Bye now."

"Bye and take care. See you Monday," Gaby said, hanging up the phone. She wondered what was going on with the usually carefree Nell. She sounded troubled about something.

I'll do what I can to help, but I wonder what she needs. Guess it'll hold until Monday.

The phone rang again just as she hung up after talking with Nell.

"Law offices, Gabriella Quinn speaking," she announced.

"Alan Waterman here. I'm wondering if I might meet with you sometime over the weekend. It's important I determine the status of Mitch's latest work. His publisher is eager to get something out while the news of Mitch's death is fresh in his readers' minds."

Chapter 15

GABY ARRANGED TO MEET WITH WATERMAN at Mitchell's cottage at one o'clock the following day. She hoped to speak with Tim before then to get his thoughts on the best approach to addressing Waterman's request. She knew it would be important to Tim for Mitchell's work-in-progress to be handled in a way that would honor his father's work.

She hoped Tim would seriously consider taking on the completion of the novel, especially since he had spent so much time with his father visiting the places that were integral to the story.

Tim called from Cambridge the next morning. "Hi, Gaby. Sorry to be calling on a Saturday, but I got in too late last night. Plus, I was exhausted. How are you?"

"So good to hear from you, Tim. I'm doing fine," Gaby answered. "How was Myrtle Beach?"

"I'm so glad I decided to go. Really did clear my head. How are things there?"

"I have a lot to catch you up on. Is now a good time?"

"Yes. Did you get ahold of Danielle?"

"That's one of the things I want to talk with you about," Gaby answered, afraid the news that St. Claire was missing would block Tim's concentration on all the other things she needed to tell him. "But first, I went ahead and changed the locks at your father's cottage. I'd like to send you a key unless you expect to be down here anytime soon."

"I'm not planning to come to Connecticut for a while. The trip really recharged my batteries. I'm thinking of taking a couple of summer courses. Lighten the course load come fall in case I decide to take a leave of absence for a semester to work on Dad's book."

"Okay. That sounds fine. I'm glad to hear you've been thinking about picking up your dad's work. So, along with the key to the cottage, I'll be sending you a form that's essentially an inventory of the estate's assets. You'll need to sign the form and send it back to me so I can file it with the court. There's a sizable 529 plan your father was using to support your studies at Harvard, as well as a good deal of money in some other accounts. That's why your father said not to worry about money."

"Wow! Mother will be happy to hear that. She's been fretting about paying the tuition bill come fall, never mind the summer session if I decide to do that. What else?"

"I've filed for an EIN for the estate," Gaby continued. "It's the equivalent of a social security number. You'll need that number to open estate accounts to pay bills as well as your tuition until the estate is settled. I'll be sending you detailed information about how to go about dealing with each of your father's accounts. A lot of it can be done online and through the mail."

"Sounds like a lot of work."

"At first, yes. But if you take it one account at a time, you'll get through it pretty quickly. Except for setting up checking accounts to take care of things that need to get paid in the coming months, there's no rush to any of it." Gaby paused, then said, "I wish I could do this for you, but it's one of the things only an executor can do."

"Okay."

"I also wanted to tell you that you'll be getting notices from the probate court as various documents are filed. They're intended to inform you of your right to request a hearing on whatever the court will be acting on. There's unlikely to be any need for you to respond to the notices or actually appear in court. If you have a question about any of them, just call me."

"Okay. That's a relief. I was wondering how I'd be able to get to the court down there if I'm still taking classes."

"This is a relatively straightforward estate, so everything can be done through the mail or, with documents like the inventory, filed electronically."

"Great. What else?"

"I'm meeting this afternoon with Alan Waterman, your father's literary agent. He wants to look through the notes and drafts of the novel your father was writing—what did you say the working title was? Warra-something?"

Tim laughed. "Warraghiyagey's Council Fire. Maybe it needs a new title."

Gaby laughed too. "I don't think so. It's provocative, interesting. I just can't seem to hold that name in my head. Anyway, Waterman says your father's publisher is eager to get something out. You've obviously given some thought to picking up where he left off; finishing what your dad started. I'm not sure how far along he was with the actual writing, but having the book completed by you would be a distinct advantage and a wonderful way to honor your father as well as his work. Is that something you'd like me to share with Waterman?"

"Like I said when we met, I'd like to try," Tim answered, "but I can't drop everything here to do that right away. That's why I was thinking about taking summer courses and then a leave of absence in the fall."

"I don't know what Waterman is thinking, but it seems to me that a press release announcing Mitchell's son will be completing the work and providing some information on the focus of the story and, perhaps, a little about your trip with your father might be what the publisher is looking for. I'd hate to see the writing done by some ghostwriter who doesn't have a feel for the material like you do."

"Hmm…"

"I was thinking I could tell Waterman you'd be open to picking up the work. That would give you time to think a little more about it rather than make a firm commitment one way or the other now."

"I like that idea. It's something I'd really like to do. I could even stay at the cottage while I do it—write where he wrote."

"Great. I'll feel my way around that with Waterman and let you know how it goes."

"Okay. By the way, did you find my dad's missing journals?"

"No, I haven't. I looked in all the likely places and came up empty. But I'm meeting on Wednesday with a woman, Karen Browning, who I hired to clean the cottage every couple of weeks. We'll be going through closets and drawers together to identify things you might want to donate or sell. The journals may turn up then."

"I'd love to have those journals if I'm going to work on Dad's novel. I know he took a lot of notes while we were away."

"I'm sure we'll find them, eventually. Now, about Danielle."

Tim's sigh could be heard on the other end of the phone. "Why do I think this is bad news?"

"I called Danielle's office like you asked. They hadn't heard from her. They checked with the place she was headed. It was in Saratoga Springs, in New York. And I learned from a friend at Mike's Place that Danielle was here that Friday evening as she had planned. Your dad was giving a talk in Pennsylvania that evening and was staying there overnight, returning to Woodson Falls early on Saturday. From what I could put together, she wasn't here when he got back."

"Did they have a fight or something?"

"I don't think he spoke with her on Friday evening. Her office asked the Royal Canadian Mounted Police to find out if she had an accident or something while she was on the road. I asked our trooper to check that as well as to see if she was in a hospital somewhere with a health problem related to the pregnancy. The problem is…"

"They came up empty?" Gaby could hear the mounting distress in Tim's voice.

"Yes. I hate telling you this over the phone, but when I was looking for the journals, I found Danielle's iPhone under the cushions of the sofa in your dad's office. I can't imagine her taking off without it, but her car wasn't parked outside, and her purse and anything else she might have brought with her for the weekend were nowhere in the cottage."

"Is she hurt? Dead, even? Tell me. Please. Just tell me."

"We just don't know, Tim. Right now, she's missing. And until we find her, she's just that. Missing."

Tim groaned. "You think she's dead, don't you?"

While Tim was right and Gaby did think St. Claire might have died somewhere between Woodson Falls and Quebec—or even here at the cottage—she said, "I just don't know, Tim. I just don't know."

Chapter 16

GABY GRABBED A QUICK LUNCH and packed her briefcase with Mitchell's financial papers and a copy of the trust document for her meeting with Alan Waterman at the cottage on Donovan's Way. She had downloaded all the files pertaining to Mitchell's current novel to a flash drive for Waterman. She still was uncertain of the extent of the relationship between Mitchell and Waterman and thought it best to prevent the agent's access to Mitchell's electronic files stored on the laptop. Granting permission for access to anything more than Mitchell's work-in-progress was Timothy's purview as executor of his father's estate.

Signaling Kat to join her, Gaby jumped into her Subaru and headed to the lakefront cottage, well ahead of her appointment with Waterman. She hadn't seen the location of the HVAC system that Eleanora had mentioned anywhere in the cottage and figured the heating system and water heater were likely in a basement beneath the house. Now she wanted to look into that space while she had bright daylight to enhance her view. Her goal was to look for signs of the possible disposal of St. Claire's body in the basement crawl space if the woman was dead as she feared, possibly killed in the cottage.

She pocketed the flash drive and left her purse and briefcase locked in her car. She'd wait until Waterman left to return the financial papers to their place in Mitchell's desk. Arriving at 9 Donovan's Way, she made her way down the slope toward the lake with Kat trailing behind her and opened the wooden door to the crawl space.

A bare light bulb hung between the furnace and the water heater. Gaby pulled on its chain. The bulb provided some dim light beyond the reach of the sun. The crawl space was small, just large enough to hold the mechanicals and the workers who had installed them. She took one of the shovels that had been left leaning against the foundation wall and probed the dirt floor, meeting resistance when she hit the bedrock on which the cottage had been built. The space was too small, and the firmly packed earth too shallow for a body to be buried here... Plus, there was no evidence that someone had disturbed the ground recently. *Just as well.* She wanted to solve the mystery of St. Claire's disappearance but wasn't sure she wanted to be the one who found the body.

She heard tires on gravel as she exited the space, turning off the light and closing the door behind her, signaling Kat to stay close. A man she assumed was Waterman emerged from a Jaguar XJ carrying a large briefcase. "Mr. Waterman?" she called as she made her way up the slope toward the cottage door.

"Attorney Quinn? Pleased to meet you."

"Likewise," she answered, "and please call me Gaby."

She recalled Eleanora saying Waterman was a "spiffy dresser," and he might well have been had he purchased clothes a size or two larger than the ill-fitting outfit he had on. He was dressed in the style of a distinguished Englishman, complete with a dark grey overcoat over a lighter grey tweed suit, a contrasting vest and black wool tie topping a button-down blue shirt. He looked instead more like an absent-minded professor—his pants drawn tight against his potbelly while the pant legs puddled at his feet. His longish drab brown hair was sprinkled with grey, his goatee a darker shade of brown. All that was missing was a derby.

Trying not to judge this book by its cover, she put on a smile and opened the cottage door. As they entered, Waterman asked, "Did you know Mitchell? I understand you've lived in Woodson Falls a while."

"I met him a few times, but I can't say I knew him well," Gaby answered. "Given what I've learned about Mitchell from his son and some of his readers, I regret that."

"Indeed," Waterman answered. "So, so sad to lose him at this point in his career. I know he had many ideas for future books. What a pity they will never see the light of day! He was quite the success in a difficult niche market."

Waterman strode across the main room, making his way to Mitchell's office, clearly familiar with the layout of the cottage. "As I told you on the phone, the publisher hopes to get something out while Mitch's name is on his fans' lips. I know it sounds crass, but that's the nature of the business. I've been hunting for a ghostwriter to finish the book Mitch was working on and wanted to gather the material he had accumulated, as well as any early drafts of the book, to give to a qualified writer. As his literary agent and trustee of his intellectual property trust, I have a duty to do justice to his final work, as I'm sure you're aware."

"Hmm... Indeed," Gaby said, having followed Waterman into the office. "Can we chat a bit about that?"

With an exaggerated look at his watch, Waterman turned to Gaby and said, "Yes. What is it you want to 'chat' about?"

Gaby sat on the leather couch while Waterman took Mitchell's seat, turning to address her while making no attempt to hide his annoyance at her interruption of his plans for the visit. Kat stood beside Gaby, looking from her to Waterman as if trying to gauge what effect this stranger was having on her owner.

"I hope you don't mind dogs. Kat's well-trained and won't bother you." *If you don't bother me.*

"Beautiful creature. Kat, hmm... Clever," Waterman replied. "No, I don't mind dogs."

Gaby smiled, hoping she looked more genuine than she felt. "I spoke with Mitchell's son Tim this morning. One of the topics we touched on was his father's work. Did you know Tim went with Mitchell on his trip to research the location of this book?"

"Hmm... No, I don't think I knew that. And?"

"Tim said he got a good feel for his father's approach to his subject. He seems to have absorbed a good deal about the focal figure in the novel. Understands the pivotal role he played in the forging of the United States as we know it today."

"You mean that illiterate Irish roughneck, Johnson? Married to a Mohawk woman?"

"Yes. Sir William Johnson, called by some 'the Mohawk baronet,'" Gaby said, recalling her conversations with Tim. "Mitchell's son thought he might try to finish his father's work. Write from here, where his father wrote, using the source materials Mitchell gathered."

"I really don't know the young man. I try to avoid getting involved with my clients' offspring. Interrupts the workflow. I understand he's in college?"

"Yes, Harvard," Gaby replied, not wanting to oversell the notion of Tim stepping into his father's creative shoes, but hoping Waterman would at least consider the idea. She knew from her career in academia before becoming an attorney that it was sometimes best to let the germ of an idea grow in the other's mind until they felt they owned it. A bit of ego-stroking usually didn't hurt either. "Of course, you'd be the best judge of the situation. Do you have a ghostwriter in mind? Someone who could pick up where Mitchell left off?"

"No, no. Not yet. I have some people to approach, but... Maybe it wouldn't be a bad idea to have the son complete the work. Certainly would appeal to his fans. I'll run it by the publisher, see what they think. The notion does have a certain allure."

"Hmm... So is there anything I can help you with?"

"Do you know where Mitch's laptop is? I'd like to see how far he got with a draft—if he got even that far. He tended to be very hush-hush about his work while he was in the midst of the writing. I knew the subject of the novel and a bit about its setting, but other than that…"

"Actually, I took the laptop for safekeeping rather than leaving it in the cottage," Gaby answered, "but I thought you might want to look at any files related to Mitchell's work-in-progress so I downloaded anything pertaining to the book to this flash drive. Since there may be other records on the laptop needed for the administration of his estate, I thought it best to let Timothy look through them before granting access to anyone else." She handed the flash drive to Waterman.

"That's reasonable. Very thoughtful of you, actually. While I'm here, though, I'd like to look through Mitch's source material to give me an idea of where he was in the project."

"I believe you'll find those files in the right-hand file drawer of the desk. When you are looking there, could you keep an eye out for his journals for this year and last? Tim was interested in reviewing them. Thought there might be jottings related to the book as well as his personal life. The journals haven't turned up in any of the likely places, but I never thought to check the files."

"Certainly," Waterman answered, offering the first smile since he had arrived as he opened the file drawer. "Mitch was a bit obsessive when he was writing. The subject consumed him, and he used whatever was at hand to make notes, so I'm sure the young lad is right, and the journals quite possibly have more than a little related to the book."

"My husband did much the same thing," Gaby said, watching as Waterman thumbed his way through the files. "I was always finding notes in odd places."

"Warraghiyagey's Council Fire," Waterman said, pulling a fat file from the desk. "Does that ring a bell? Mitch never revealed the working title of the book to me. Didn't want to commit to it and then have to change it."

"That would be it. It's a mouthful, but it grows on you," Gaby said. "I'll leave you to it. I need to organize things in the sunroom. Just give me a shout when you're done."

Chapter 17

AN HOUR OR MORE HAD PASSED before Gaby heard Waterman call to her, saying he had concluded his search for materials related to Mitchell's latest work. He was standing at the office door as she made her way toward him from the sunroom.

"I've got what I need, I believe," he said. "I can always contact you again, I suppose, if I need to reengage with Mitch's material."

"Of course," Gaby replied. "By the way, did you come across Mitchell's journals during your search?"

"No, no sign of them," he answered. "I'll use the flash drive you so kindly provided to review the draft Mitch had completed. I'm leaving everything else here, though. The notion of Mitch's son completing the manuscript is intriguing, and I think I can sell it to the publisher if the lad is serious about doing the work. Fortunately, Mitch was a plotter by nature and had developed a detailed outline of the novel—start to finish—which I found in the files. It could serve as a roadmap for the individual picking up the work where he left off.

"I'll have to look at the actual draft, but based on what Mitch told me, he'd completed more than half of the planned manuscript. Of course, we'll never know what serendipitous thoughts might have occurred to him while he was writing—things that might have taken him 'off course' and down a side path, so to speak. Those little asides can add a level of charm to the work. But that can't be helped.

"The real issue is capturing Mitch's unique style—his literary 'voice' as they put it in the writing world. Very much part of what made his novels so popular. That's what's most compelling about the son picking up the work. He certainly knew his father's spoken voice, which just might be what's needed for him to pick up Mitch's literary style. It's certainly one of the things I'll be emphasizing to the publisher."

"Do you have Tim's contact information? I know the trust document indicates any unpaid distribution due to Mitchell was to be paid over to Tim free of trust, so I imagine you'll need to connect with him about that as well as to get his social security number. And if the publisher does agree with you about giving Tim the opportunity to complete his father's work, I'm sure there will be some sort of contract involved. That is, of course, if Tim decides to pursue the opportunity."

"The more I think about it, I certainly hope he'll seriously consider it. Mitch's fans would view it favorably, and the news would create the level of buzz the publisher is looking for."

"Well, I'll communicate your thoughts to Tim. Unless you would prefer pursuing this with him yourself?"

"I think at this stage the communication would be best coming from you. Down the line, perhaps we three could get together, perhaps after Mitch's memorial service once it's finally scheduled. Discuss where Tim might be in his thinking about slipping into his father's shoes."

Gaby found it odd Waterman hadn't mentioned St. Claire or asked how she was taking Mitchell's death. She also wondered whether Mitchell had told Waterman that he was planning to marry Danielle, and how the agent might have reacted to that news. Gaby took this opportunity to probe a bit about that.

"Mitchell also made a provision for Danielle St. Claire in the trust agreement. Did he talk to you about her? He had expected Danielle to be at the cottage when he returned from his speaking engage-ment in Scranton. It seems no one knows what's become of her. The people at her travel agency up in Quebec haven't heard from her in over a month."

"Hmm… Well, yes, Mitch did mention something about her not being here when he came home. I had been invited to join them for dinner but had other obligations. I'm sure she'll turn up, eventually. Flighty little thing. Not sure what Mitch saw in her, especially since she's so much younger than he."

"Would you let me know if you hear from her?"

"Of course."

"Do you need anything else from me at this time?"

"No, I think I'm okay. Thanks for your time and for thinking of downloading the files for the novel and bringing the flash drive. Very helpful," Waterman said, picking up his still-empty briefcase and heading toward the door. "I'll let you know what the publisher thinks about young Timothy taking over the project. I'm confident I can sell them on the idea."

"I'll let Tim know what we've discussed and get back to you with his thoughts," Gaby said.

Returning to the cottage after Waterman left, Gaby returned the financial papers to their place in the left-hand desk drawer now that she was sure she had captured all the details necessary for the probate court filings.

When she met Karen Browning at the cottage on Wednesday, she planned to search for any clues in the cottage pointing to the fate of Danielle St. Claire, so she didn't feel the need to look around the cottage any more now. Thinking about it, she was glad she hadn't found evidence of the woman's burial in the dirt basement. Why on earth had she thought she could conduct the search on her own?

Satisfied she had accomplished her goal for the meeting with Waterman, Gaby locked up the cottage and returned home. She hoped to get some gardening in before night fell. She had already brought a good half of her spacious garden under some semblance of control, despite having her weekends interrupted by meetings with Eleanora, Tim and now Alan Waterman. Time would tell, but she sensed she had made significant progress and wanted to complete the job before the plants burst forward with the arrival of warmer weather.

Gaby was in the kitchen heating dinner after taking a much-needed shower. She had accomplished her goal of completing work on the garden; her dirt-encrusted fingernails, hands and knees were evidence of her efforts. She hoped that Nell could give her guidance on next steps when she came for lunch on Monday. Gaby had spoken with Tim before changing into her gardening clothes. He seemed excited at the prospect of picking up his father's work and told her she was free to communicate this to Waterman.

She was about to prepare Kat's meal when the phone rang. "Law offices, Gabriella Quinn speaking."

A strident Eleanora was at the other end of the line. "Where is the key to the cottage?" she shrieked. "I've looked all over, and I can't find it."

"The locks have been changed, Mrs. Mitchell. It was…"

"Does my son know about this?" she screamed into the phone. "How dare you lock him out of his own father's home!"

"Of course Tim knows. I talked with him about safeguarding the cottage and about changing the locks since many people knew where Mr. Mitchell kept the key. Tim has a new key."

"But I need to get in there now!" Eleanora retorted.

"It's really not appropriate for you to be in the cottage without either me or your son now that Tim has control of his father's property as executor of his estate. Why would you need to get into the cottage?"

"But I'm his mother," Eleanora whined, ignoring Gaby's question.

"Yes, but you have no legal interest in the estate now that your son has been appointed executor," Gaby responded.

"Clothes. I need to pick out clothes for the funeral."

"I thought Tim said his father had been cremated. Or am I mistaken?"

"I… I need to return Mitch's journals. I took them to help with the obituary, and I thought they should be with the others."

"So that's where the journals went! Tim was so upset when he couldn't find them. Does he know you had them?"

"No, I don't think he does," a subdued Eleanora answered. "He never asked me."

"Why don't I run down there? I'll meet you at the cottage and return the journals to the office bookshelf. Tim will be so relieved to learn they've been found."

"No bother. They're in a plastic bag. I'll just hang the bag on the doorknob and that will be that. I need to get back to the city."

"It may rain tonight. I'll come down to the cottage and get them inside," Gaby answered. "You could wait for me if you really feel you need to get into the cottage for something else."

"No, no. I'll be on my way. I do need to get back to New York."

Gaby shook her head, looking at the phone in her hand. Eleanora had hung up without bothering to say goodbye.

"Guess we'll both be postponing dinner tonight, Kat," she said as she shrugged into a jacket. "Let's go."

Even though her stomach was growling after her garden exertions, Gaby didn't want anything to happen to the journals and so returned to Donovan's Way to get them back on the bookshelf. They were in a plastic bag and hanging from the doorknob, as Eleanora had said, but they wouldn't have been protected from the rain threatening to pour later in the evening. Putting the journals back on the shelf next to the others, Gaby locked up the cottage again. She was heading toward her car when she noticed a faint light shining on the lawn below and made her way down toward the dock.

The basement door was open, and the light was on. *I'm sure I turned that light off and secured the door before meeting Waterman.*

Gaby took a peek into the basement crawl space. Except for a sprinkling of lime she hadn't noticed before, most likely from the bag leaning against the foundation wall, nothing seemed to be disturbed. Shrugging her shoulders, Gaby turned off the light, shut the door, and went back home.

Chapter 18

GABY MET NELL ON THE FLAGSTONE WALKWAY when she arrived for lunch on Monday. Nell was gazing at the garden, surveying Gaby's work. It had warmed up considerably over the weekend; the sun was shining brightly through the pine trees fronting Gaby's property. Growth in the garden seemed to have accelerated overnight.

"Looks like you made a lot of headway on this project," Nell said, smiling at Gaby. "Certainly made enough room for things to grow. It's still early in the season, but from what I can see poking up, you did a good job."

"Thanks for the 'atta girl.' Guess I'll have a better idea come July, when armies of plants will be at war battling for space."

"The trick is to keep up with the growth. I know you're busy, but as I suggested before, if you just take an hour each weekend, you should be able to tame the growth into the beautiful cottage garden you've wanted. Time will tell.

"If you find yourself with some empty spots to fill, try annuals. You can pick them based on the color scheme you find pleasing. I can see some rudbeckia leaves poking through, but you won't know until later in the season whether they're black-eyed Susan or purple coneflower. Same family, but a totally different look. And it looks like you have several varieties of coreopsis, which may be bright yellow or more orange in tone. They also vary in height and size of the blossom.

"A lot of gardeners keep a diary to remind themselves of what they have and when something is likely to appear. Pictures are helpful as well in tracking a garden's progress while you're still learning."

"Good suggestions. That would be a fun way to learn and coax the garden into becoming something I'm proud of."

"Exactly."

They walked up the path and into the cottage.

"Thanks for inviting me for lunch, Gaby."

"My pleasure. Anytime. But I have to confess, you've got me worried. Is everything okay?"

"With me? Yes. Couldn't be better. I just need a big favor, and it requires some explanation; things I'd rather keep private."

"Anything, Nell. You know that. Would you like to talk first or have lunch? I've prepared a simple salad, which can wait if you prefer."

"Perhaps talk first. Maybe over a glass of wine, if you wouldn't be opposed to drinking midday?"

"No problem. I have a lovely sauvignon blanc in the refrigerator. Why don't you get settled in the den, and I'll bring the wine?"

After they had clinked glasses and each taken a sip of wine, Nell began.

"Of course, you know I practiced personal injury law in New York City before coming to Woodson Falls. A lawyer in that field risks being labeled an ambulance chaser, but I was good at it. People who might otherwise be anxious about dealing with an attorney, especially after being injured, seemed to trust me."

"Oh, of course they would, Nell. You're super-smart, but you're also so warm and accessible. You connect with people. It's a rare combination for an attorney."

"And one we share, I think. Anyway, after I graduated from law school at Fordham, I landed a job at a prominent New York firm, Fordyce & Whitney. I worked hard—paid my dues, so to speak—and was mostly successful. That brought me to the attention of the founding partners, who directed a good number of difficult but lucrative cases my way. Before long—actually in record time—I was made partner and earned a sizable share of the firm's income.

"Along the way, I caught the eye of David Whitney, son of one of the founders. We were married after a whirlwind courtship, much to the approval of his father. We were young, well-launched in our careers, and deeply in love. The stars seemed aligned in our favor—at least in our first years of marriage."

Nell paused, took a sip of her wine, and looked out the window.

"I knew you had been married, but you never told me what happened with your husband, whether he had died or you divorced. I guess I was too wrapped up in my own misery to even think to ask you. What happened?" Gaby prompted.

"I'd always wanted children. David was lukewarm on the subject but willing to agree after the first few years of our marriage. I had our son Joshua first, a beautiful boy. Took after his father. We were well off, able to hire a nanny to care for Josh during the day, so I went back to work after a short maternity leave. Two years later, I had Jacquelyn. With her birth, the tug between my love of the law and my deep desire to be with the children left me feeling frayed at the edges. I still churned out the work, but my heart was less engaged with the law and increasingly filled with a longing to be with the children."

Nell mustered a smile through tears that were threatening to spill as she took another sip of wine before continuing.

"It had been relatively easy to hand a fussy baby to a nanny and head out the door. But it was much harder to kiss a clinging toddler goodbye, never mind two of them. The children's sobs as I left each day followed me to the office and began to interfere with my work. As my productivity decreased, the flow of assignments gradually shifted and associates were being handed the plum assignments that had always been mine. It hurt, especially since it was my father-in-law—the children's grandfather—who was doling out the work. I took it personally, as a criticism not only of my productivity as an attorney but also of my mothering skills. Silly, I know, but that's how I felt."

Unsure of how this story related to the favor Nell was going to ask of her, Gaby sensed it was important to let Nell frame her request in her own way.

Chapter 19

"WHERE WAS DAVID in all of this?" she asked, inviting her friend to continue.

"Missing in action, to tell the truth. David was a corporate litigator, much sought after by major commercial companies seeking to prosecute or defend contractual issues. My practice was based in the city, while David's required a good bit of traveling. As I became more focused on the children, I missed the signs of our marriage dissolving. David was out late most evenings, working over weekends, away more than he was home. I was shocked when he served me with divorce papers, but in reality, I should have seen it coming.

"We'd grown apart. He never really bonded with the children to the degree I had, and they became the unwitting wedge between us. When the divorce was finalized, I was granted sole custody of the children. David agreed to a substantial support obligation, which he always fulfilled. Although he had visitation rights, he rarely saw the children or even asked about them in our infrequent contacts."

"Did you continue with the law?"

"Yes. The firm couldn't remove me as partner, although my share in the firm's income declined along with my productivity. I did eventually leave the firm and signed on with an insurance company. The children were in school by that time, and I was able to arrange my schedule around theirs."

"And that worked for you?" Gaby asked, pouring a second glass of wine for each of them.

"For the most part. As the children grew up, they were less dependent on me, more engaged with their friends. I began to miss the thrill of the win I had experienced earlier in my career, while at the same time starting to view the law as more of a burden than a pleasure." Nell smiled. "I was not in a good place, especially once the kids left home for college."

"Is that how you came to live in Woodson Falls?"

"Not immediately, but yes. I ended up so filled with self-doubt about the choices I had made that I finally sought the help of a therapist. The support she provided enabled me to recognize I was more than an attorney or a mother—I could pretty much transform myself into whatever I wanted."

"Sort of the reverse of my journey, from teaching philosophy and into the law," Gaby said, recognizing she, too, had re-invented herself after the traumatizing events surrounding Joe's death.

"Exactly! I started by dabbling in this and that. Acquiring both useful and useless knowledge. The New Age stuff appealed to me. It was totally different, almost counter to the logical, methodical approach of the law. It was, at least for me, engaging in its own way and very calming. And the thrill of the win returned when I realized it was there in finding unique items I could share with others. That's what led me to the store and, ultimately, to Woodson Falls."

"Well, I, for one, am glad you landed here. I don't know where I'd be without our friendship—and your guidance and assistance."

"I'm glad. Anyway, to continue the saga, David's obligation of financial support ended once the children were launched. Over time, we had become friends again. David's a very likable person, and that didn't change for me just because we no longer were partners. He also grew closer to the children once they were adults.

"We were both quite wealthy, and we both were experiencing the tax issues wealth can create. On one occasion, when we were discussing the kids, we decided it would be in our best interests and theirs to provide some ongoing financial backing for each of them through a trust arrangement rather than have them wait for an inheritance farther down the line. At the same time, substantial funding of the trusts would reduce our tax burdens both now and, in terms of estate taxes, upon our deaths. We ended up establishing separate trusts for Jacquelyn and Joshua, with the two of us serving as co-trustees."

"I knew you had adult children, although you don't talk much about them," Gaby said. "I remember meeting your daughter and grandchildren, but not your son. Do they live in the area? Do you see them often?"

"They're both nearby. I see Jacqueline more than Josh, but I love them both dearly." Nell took a deep breath and another sip of wine. "Why don't we have lunch while I lay out the issues I'm facing."

Gaby had prepared one of her favorite meals for guests: a springtime salad consisting of sesame shrimp over sugar snap peas. The pair wandered into the kitchen, where Gaby brought the platter of peas and shrimp out of the refrigerator. She drizzled a simple lemon-sesame dressing over the top, then sprinkled the salad with toasted sesame seeds and sliced scallions.

"What a lovely dish!" Nell exclaimed, taking a seat at the kitchen table, while Gaby served the salad.

"Enjoy!" she said. "And please continue."

Taking a bite of shrimp, Nell swallowed, then said, "Delicious! You're such a gifted cook!"

Nell took a few more bites of the salad before continuing.

"Jacquelyn is married with three delightful children who I adore. The problem with Jackie is her husband, who's a spendthrift. Her trust is designed to support both her and her children, while denying access to the funds by her husband Ed, especially if they were to divorce down the line. Of course, once Jackie receives a distribution from the trust, there's no way to control how it's spent. Ed's very much into antique cars. Claims he's restoring them for resale, but they just keep accumulating, and I worry that Ed pressures Jackie to support his hobby rather than put the money toward the children's education or her own desire to be an artist.

"Worse than that, though… Joshua is my problem child—or rather, my problem young man. He started smoking pot in college and has progressed to narcotics, the opiates legitimately prescribed for his supposed back pain following a biking accident, and now and then street drugs. He also drinks heavily on occasion. Josh works on and off in sales—cars, insurance, whatever he can land. He'll do well for a while, then fall off the wagon. I can't tell you how many times David and I have paid for stays in one or another rehab facility. He's been living, off and on, with a woman, Elaine, who I think is an enabler or co-dependent. Of course, giving him access to the trust funds has the potential to fuel his drug habit."

"Oh my! I never knew. You've kept that a secret. It must be difficult for you."

"Not really hard at all. I haven't told a soul here in Woodson Falls about my family issues, so nobody asks. I'm sure they think I'm either a widow or spinster, puttering around a store that's likely a losing proposition and struggling to make ends meet. I don't care about that. But I do care about the children and grandchildren and want so very much to do the right thing for them.

"Here's the problem: David is remarrying and wants to resign as trustee of the trusts. I certainly understand that. But it's been David who's been best able to stand firm when he feels either Jacquelyn or Joshua might be taking advantage of our generosity, requesting additional distributions from their trusts beyond the required annual distributions under their terms. I'm a softie, and I'm concerned the children will take advantage of that. David was the one who dealt with their requests. I took care of the accounting and management of the trust assets."

"I don't understand," Gaby said. "What's the problem, and how can I help?"

Chapter 20

"I'D LIKE YOU TO SERVE AS CO-TRUSTEE of the children's trusts; take David's position in terms of determining whether additional funds should be paid out to Jackie or Josh if either of them requests it. I'd continue to do the bookkeeping, tax work and reporting, but you'd be the person they'd interact with regarding the trust."

"And you think I have the backbone for that? The ability to say 'no' to either of your children?"

"Absolutely! I've known you since you arrived back in Woodson Falls. You may not realize this, but you've grown in confidence over time. You're committed to doing the right thing, and you've got a good moral compass for evaluating a situation. Plus, you understand how trusts work and can answer any questions the kids have along the way. They take what I say from the perspective of me being their mom. And they learned a long time ago that I'm a softie where they're concerned."

"I'd be honored to serve as a co-trustee, especially with you, but I've only met your daughter in passing and never your son. Do they know David is resigning as co-trustee?"

"They do. They also know I had planned to ask you to serve in that role and would like to get together with us to understand the changes that will occur with the management of distributions from the trust. We can set something up when you're available."

"That would be great."

"One other thing. I'm a good twenty years older than you are. I'm healthy as an ox, but you never know. I'd like you to continue as trustee when I'm gone. Otherwise, a bank's trust department would take over, and I can't abide the fees they charge. I looked into that when David told me he would be resigning. I'd really prefer to work with you."

"Okay. I just hope you know what you're doing. I appreciate the confidence you have in me, but I'm not sure I'm as strong-willed as you think I am."

"Believe me. You are."

"Well, thank you—I guess. It's a big obligation, but I'll do my best."

"I know you will, and you'll succeed."

The friends finished eating, chatting about this and that. Nell described a big sale she'd made of some jewelry she'd taken on consignment but thought would never sell while Gaby filled her in on the puzzle created by St. Claire's disappearance. They finished their meal with jasmine tea and almond cookies.

"Thanks so much for lunch and for agreeing to take on the trusts, Gaby."

"So lovely to have you over, Nell."

Gaby accompanied her friend as she left, both pausing to look at the garden again.

"You might want to consider amending the soil," Nell said.

"What do you mean?"

"With these pines and the wood mulch in the garden, the soil may have grown acidic over time. Look for the annual soil tests the agriculture extension offers around this time of year. Or pick one up at a gardening center. The test will tell you the pH of the soil. It matters with some plants more than others, but increasing the pH of the soil can help with bloom."

"How do you do that?"

"Lime works. Not much. Just a sprinkling, preferably before the garden is in full bloom. You might also want to put down a thin layer of rotted manure."

"That sounds gross!"

"It isn't, surprisingly. There's no odor. In any event, lime would suppress any odors, but there are none with rotted manure. Just be sure to wear gloves. You never know if tetanus spores are mixed in with the manure. They live forever."

Nell turned and gave Gaby a big hug. "I'm so glad we're friends. And I'm so happy we had this time together."

"Me too, Nell. You've helped me in so many ways. This gives me a chance to give something back to you."

Chapter 21

WOODSON FALLS TOWN HALL WASN'T OPEN on Mondays, so Gaby couldn't check on the issues that had arisen with Winston Pinkham's subdivision application. Instead, she continued to work through the pile on her desk after Nell had left. The next day she stopped in at Mike's Place for a quick breakfast before Town Hall opened.

"Hi, Gaby," Emma greeted her as she stepped up to the deli. "No Danish left, I'm afraid. What'll it be?"

"A buttered roll, I guess. And coffee, black. Thanks."

"Here's the coffee. I'll bring the roll over. I have something I want to tell you."

Gaby brought her coffee over to a table, letting the brew cool a bit before Emma sat down beside her.

"Remember when you were asking me if I had seen any of Mr. Mitchell's lady friends a while back?"

"Yes. You were helpful. I found the ingredients his Quebec friend had purchased to make the dinner she had planned. You were right. Her name is Danielle St. Claire."

"Well, I remembered I saw Mr. Mitchell's ex-wife that same day."

"Really? That's odd. She works in the city, and I got the impression from talking with her that she preferred it to Woodson Falls. Too quiet for her. Plus, it's an hour-and-a-half drive—one way. Yet she was here Saturday evening too. She wanted to get into Mitchell's cottage, but I had changed the locks."

"Well, I've seen her here now and then, and I recall seeing her that day. I'm not sure whether it was before or after I saw the Quebec lady, but it was definitely the same day. I remember thinking it would be awkward for them both if they ran into each other."

"Interesting."

"Anything else going on?"

"Just work," Gaby responded, not wanting to tell Emma about St. Claire's disappearance. "And I've gotten a good start on the garden I'm trying to bring back to life."

Emma returned to the deli to serve yet another customer while Gaby munched on her roll, wondering why Eleanora Mitchell was visiting Woodson Falls so often. Thinking back to the sprinkling of lime she had seen in the cottage crawl space, Gaby speculated Eleanora might have been sweetening the soil around the shrubs fronting the cottage. Perhaps she was providing a bit of maintenance so Tim would have a better chance of getting a good price when he put the place on the market, as she assumed he would.

As Woodson Falls' land use clerk, Miriam Henderson was responsible for all land use activities on properties in the town that required permits. Her comprehensive files on each property included zoning, building and health permits as well as wetlands permits when the property required these. Besides this work, Miriam taped the proceedings of the various land use commissions in town, transcribing the minutes, and then filing them in the town records once they were approved.

"Good morning, Miriam," Gaby said as she entered the busy clerk's office. "Would you have a few minutes to help me make sense of Winston Pinkham's subdivision application for Sunrise Hills?"

"Sure, Gaby," she answered, pulling out a file and a map from the pile sitting on the corner of her desk. "I was just finishing organizing things for this evening's planning and zoning commission meeting, so everything's handy."

"Bill Harrison talked with me the other day. He seems to think there have been unnecessary delays in getting the application approved."

"You can say that again! But it's not the commission's fault. These land use experts seem to be introducing wrinkles with every modification they submit."

"That was Bill's impression, too. He's tried to warn Mr. Pinkham, but so far Pinkham hasn't wanted to intervene. I discussed the situation with him myself, and he agreed to have me observe tonight's meeting and give him my impressions."

Miriam showed Gaby some of the subtle changes made to the plan—changes that violated one or another land use regulation. After pointing out what was likely to happen at the evening's meeting, she said, "I'm glad people are looking out for Mr. Pinkham. It ought to be a crime to take advantage of older folks like him."

"Actually, it is," Gaby responded. "I'll see you this evening. Ought to be interesting."

With nothing much else to attend to, Gaby decided to spend some time at 9 Donovan's Way in an attempt to organize things before Karen Browning arrived to do the cleaning. She wanted to spare Tim some of the pain involved with going through a loved one's possessions after they died.

She picked up some empty cardboard boxes from Mike's Place. She had a Sharpie in her car's glove compartment that would come in handy in labeling boxes. There were contractor's bags under the kitchen sink.

Gaby began with the downstairs bedroom where it seemed Mitchell was living except when St. Claire was here. She speculated that he might have preferred being close to the office when he was in the midst of his writing, not wanting to waste any time going downstairs when a new thought hit him, especially given the need to strap on his artificial leg before hazarding the stairs. Waterman had said the writer was prone to serendipitous thoughts that spiced up his work.

She planned to keep an eye out for anything that could point to where St. Claire might be, but based on her earlier search, she didn't think she'd find much. Her chief goal was to pack up most of the clothing and other personal stuff Tim might want to go through in the future and discard the day-to-day items—toothpaste, shampoo— things like that. She had used some of the time when Waterman was here to organize the sunroom a bit. She planned to store things for Tim there, using the Sharpie to mark each box so he'd get a sense of the contents. That way, he could decide what to keep and what to donate or discard without the pain of going through it piece by piece.

She wasn't quite sure what to do with Mitchell's spare artificial leg. That would be too much for anyone, even Tim. Same with the artificial eye she found lying on the bedside table. She put both in a separate box labeled "Prostheses" and added it to the pile in the sunroom.

Heading upstairs, she packed up the items clearly belonging to Mitchell and leaving St. Claire's for her possible return to the cottage. Her work over the next few hours provided plenty of space for Tim or St. Claire to occupy the cottage if either chose to do so. If Tim decided to put it on the market instead, she had made a significant dent in the amount of packing to be done to prepare the house for sale.

But even after looking in all the cottage's nooks and crannies, Gaby found no clues pointing to St. Claire's disappearance.

Chapter 22

GABY SLIPPED INTO A CHAIR in the back of the meeting room just before the members of the planning and zoning commission arrived and took their seats at the front table. The room was packed with people interested in one or another item on the agenda. Gaby recalled her own attendance at one of these meetings when she was renovating her grandparents' cottage. People tended to leave after their cases were heard, the audience dwindling in size though occasionally supplemented by newcomers whose cases were further down the agenda.

She spotted Bill Harrison with a group of four men. Gaby assumed the two men in business suits seated beside Bill were the developers. Two other men in more casual clothes were seated just behind them, leaning forward to chat with the men Gaby thought were the developers. Bill nodded to her, acknowledging her arrival but recognizing she wanted to observe the meeting without her presence being evident to the men representing Pinkham's subdivision application.

As the meeting droned on, Gaby's thoughts drifted to where she might look for signs of St. Claire's location if she was still alive, or her body if—as Gaby suspected—she had been killed. *But who would do such a thing, and why?* Her attention returned to the meeting when the chair announced consideration of the latest modifications to the Sunrise Hills subdivision plan.

"We see you made the modifications we told you would bring this proposed subdivision into conformity with the regulations," the commission chair began, "but note that other changes have been made that are non-conforming. This item has been on our agenda for several months now, and we're wondering what prompted these latest changes when we were so close to approving the subdivision plan?" The other commissioners nodded, then sat back in their chairs as one of the men seated beside Harrison stood.

"Good evening, gentlemen, ladies," he began. "If it pleases the commission, we have made every effort to bring this subdivision into conformity with the town's regulations. However, we had to take into consideration the salability of the individual lots on this difficult terrain."

"A laudable goal," the commission chair responded, "but not our concern, as I'm sure you understand. We recognize it's a balancing act for the developer, but in the end, the regulations will always trump any esthetic concerns. Now, here's where the non-conformities were introduced and need to be corrected."

The chair went through the map that accompanied the application lot by lot, explaining where modifications made by the developer violated one or another of the planning or zoning regulations.

"Understood?" he asked, clearly frustrated with the developers.

"Understood, sir. We'll have the modifications ready for your next meeting."

"Good. I'd like to have this application approved and off our agenda before summer. I'm sure Mr. Pinkham, who you represent in this matter, would like that as well."

"Yes, sir," the developer responded respectfully, rolling up his map and signaling his partner, Harrison and the two other men—most likely Pinkham's friends—to join him in the hall as he exited the meeting.

Gaby rose from her seat and made her way to the hallway as the chair announced, "Moving on to new business…"

"May I have a word with you, gentlemen?" she asked, addressing the developers and ignoring Pinkham's friends.

"Of course," said the man who had spoken on behalf of the subdivision. "You are?"

"Gabriella Quinn. I hold Mr. Pinkham's power of attorney and am here as his agent and at his request to determine the degree to which his interests are being represented by your firm."

"Excuse me?"

One of Pinkham's friends interrupted before the developer could go on. "Whaddaya mean? Me and Bud are here to represent Pinky's interests."

Gaby turned to the two men, who looked a bit like a modern-day Mutt and Jeff, one tall and slim and the other short and portly. "You are?"

Sticking out his hand to Gaby, the taller man said, "Adam Samuelson, and this here's Pinky's other friend, Bud Wiseman. We told Pinky we'd watch out for him since he doesn't feel up to attending these meetings. He never mentioned you."

Ignoring Samuelson's proffered hand, Gaby said, "I'll speak with you both later, after I've had a chance to talk to these gentlemen," then turned back to the two men from the engineering firm.

"Perhaps we can go down to the conference room," she said to the developers, ignoring the friends, who started to follow them. Gaby stopped, turning toward them. "Adam, Bud. I'd like to speak with these gentlemen and Mr. Pinkham's attorney privately. I'll talk with you after I'm done with them."

Adam moved toward Gaby, but Harrison put a hand on his shoulder and said, "Please listen to the lady. She'll get back to you in just a bit."

Once they were settled in the conference room, Gaby asked, "Just what prompted the latest changes? Mr. Pinkham would like to move ahead with the subdivision and sell the lots. He's concerned about the money he's spending on this and whether he'll be able to recapture it once the lots are sold. The many delays in gaining approval of this plan are just costing him more money and delaying him in reaching his ultimate goal of monetizing the land he owns."

"It's those yokels out there," said the developer's partner. "They're focused on the lots Pinkham said he'd sell to them at a discount and keep asking for changes that enlarge the lots or improve a view or some-such. We took them at their word that they were representing Pinkham's interests, but I can see how that could be misinterpreted."

"Did you ever verify their claims with Mr. Pinkham?"

"Uh, no. We did not."

"And what do you think those 'yokels' will claim about your role in these delays?"

"How would we know?" the partner responded indignantly.

"Take a guess."

"Probably that we're manufacturing excuses to keep this subdivision on the commission's agenda. But that's patently false."

"I have a feeling there's plenty of blame on both sides. In any event, it's clear Pinkham's interests are not in the forefront for any of you. It's time for that to change. Financial abuse of the elderly is against the law, and while there would be a good deal to unravel to convict you all of such a crime, there's more than enough to support charges of elder abuse. I imagine that wouldn't be beneficial to your firm's reputation."

The partners looked at each other, then the apparent spokesman said, "We'll need a minute to talk this over."

"No problem. I'll be down the hall with those two 'friends' of Pinkham's."

Gaby left the room, quietly closing the door behind her. *Guess Nell is right. I have developed a backbone. It's just so wrong, what they're doing to Mr. Pinkham.*

Approaching Adam and Bud, Gaby wondered just how they were connected to Pinkham. They didn't seem at all like the type of people he would be associated with. But he must have had a reason. She said,

"I know Mr. Pinkham promised to sell each of you a lot of your choice in this subdivision at a discount in return for your help with getting the plans approved. And I know Mr. Pinkham is a man of his word. However, I'm beginning to wonder just whose interests you're here to represent—his or your own."

"Now listen here, Ms...." Adam began.

"Quinn. Gabriella Quinn," she answered. "Attorney Quinn."

"Of course, we want what's best for Pinky, Ms. Quinn. We're trying to do just that."

"Well, for one reason or another, it's not working, so I'm going to advise you now that the subdivision plan submitted to the next commission meeting will conform to each and every regulation. That's what's best for Mr. Pinkham."

"It won't be our fault if it doesn't."

"Make sure of that, or I'll proceed with my suspicion that you both are engaged in elder abuse. Clear?"

"Yeah, yeah. We hear you," Adam said, turning to Bud. "Come on, Bud. Let's get a beer and call it a night."

The pair sauntered down the hall as if they'd just won a battle Gaby knew they had lost while she went back to the conference room to complete her discussion with the developers.

Bill Harrison rose as she entered the room. "We think we've arrived at a resolution of this matter, Attorney Quinn," he said. "These gentlemen from Blackberry Hill Engineering have agreed to remove the non-conformities introduced into the last subdivision plan. That should satisfy the commission and achieve the goal of gaining full approval of the plan at the commission's next meeting. And they have assured me the revised plan will be submitted well in advance of the deadline so the item can appear earlier in the meeting."

"Well, that sounds like a satisfactory resolution of the issues. I'll be happy to report that to Mr. Pinkham when I meet with him tomorrow, and I'll be in attendance at the next meeting of the commission.

Gentlemen, Attorney Harrison, have a good evening," Gaby said, shaking hands with each of them.

"Can I speak with you on another matter, Attorney Quinn?" Harrison asked, ushering Gaby out the door. Once they were in the hallway and out of hearing of the engineers, he said, "Well played, Gaby. Well played. And thank you."

"I just hope those bozos carry through. I'd hate to have to litigate this. That would only serve to delay the matter further and cost Pinkham more money."

"They will. I'll make sure of it."

"Good, and good night, Bill," she said with a smile, leaving the building with a feeling of strength as well as satisfaction with the outcome of the evening's events.

Chapter 23

"I BROUGHT YOU SOME ALMOND COOKIES," Gaby called to Winston Pinkham from the foyer when she visited him the next morning. "I'll put them in the kitchen. I made a batch for lunch with a friend, but there were more than we could eat ourselves."

As she came into the living room, she stood in front of Pinkham, shaking her head. He was seated in his usual wingback chair. The nasal cannula he should be wearing hung around his neck while the concentrator delivering oxygen to the tubing chugged away in the background. Pinkham took a long drag of his cigarette before stubbing it out in the ashtray at his side, already filled with cigarette butts.

"I know, I know," he said to Gaby with a guilty smile, securing the prongs of the nasal cannula into his nostrils. "It may be a filthy habit, but it's mine to enjoy. So don't say a word."

"I won't," she replied, sitting beside him. "You wouldn't listen, anyway."

"So, did you attend last night's commission meeting?"

"I did. And I spoke with the land use experts from Blackberry Hill Engineering who presented the plan for Sunrise Hills as well as with your friends, Adam and Bud."

"Everything hunky-dory?"

"Not really. Attorney Harrison is right. There have been deliberate delays by either Blackberry Hill or your friends or possibly both that have run up development costs unnecessarily. The people from Blackberry Hill agreed to return the plan to a form that will win approval at the next commission meeting so the project can move ahead before the snow falls."

"Is it really that bad?" Pinkham asked.

"Sorry to say it is," Gaby replied. "Even the commission chair was annoyed with all the delays and apparent shenanigans."

"Now I feel like a complete idiot."

"You shouldn't. The regulatory issues are complex, and I would bet that few engineering firms in the country would get a subdivision plan for your land right the first time. I wouldn't have been able to understand what was going on if Bill Harrison hadn't alerted me to the possible issues and if I hadn't taken the time to go over the plan with the land use clerk."

"So, what should I do? Do I need to start over?"

"No, not at all. You really don't need to do anything. I took a chance in deciding to talk things over with the developers as well as with Adam and Bud. The Blackberry Hill people agreed to fix changes that introduced the latest non-conformities and submit a revised plan likely to win approval at the next meeting. I'll be attending that meeting to make sure they do as they've agreed. Adam and Bud seemed to understand that the plan the engineers present next time is what will be used moving forward. I think it will all work out."

"What would I do without you, Gaby?"

"Oh, you'd be fine. It's just a shame these people took advantage of the situation, even after Bill voiced his concerns to them. It took another voice, which happened to be mine, to get things on the right path."

Gaby headed back to her cottage after leaving Pinkham's house on Sunrise Trail. She hoped to get some work in before meeting Karen Browning at 9 Donovan's Way. Continuing her work on the Bryant's estate plan, she managed to complete a first draft of the required documents. She planned to review them when she returned home after meeting with Karen, who was waiting for her when she arrived at Mitchell's cottage. She left Kat in the car while she met with the young woman.

"Thanks so much, Karen. I'm hoping to get the place in some kind of order before Mitchell's girlfriend or son wants to use it."

"No problem, Gaby. Happy to have the work. The post office has been cutting back my hours. Still have my benefits, but frankly, anything extra coming in is more than welcome. You said Rusty Dolan recommended me?"

Gaby nodded as she opened the cottage door and let Karen precede her into the house.

"I'll have to thank him when I see him next. Wow! This is nice! I've never been in one of these cottages. It's like you're on a houseboat!"

"Different, don't you think? I had some extra time yesterday and spent a few hours putting Mitchell's belongings in boxes that I stored in the sunroom for his son to go through when he's back here. What I'm hoping to have done today is a basic cleaning of the place. It's just this level and upstairs. There's a crawl space containing the mechanicals, but no basement to speak of. Sorry. I never checked to see if there are cleaning supplies stashed someplace."

"No problem. I've taken to storing the basics in the trunk of my car. I used to be a Girl Scout. Always prepared," she answered with a smile.

"I think Mitchell had regular garbage service, judging from the bins that are up at the end of the driveway. It's been about a month since he passed away, so I know the refrigerator and, probably, the freezer should be emptied and cleaned. Other than that and obvious trash, you'll probably want to leave any 'deep cleaning' for another time. So, just the basics today."

"Sounds fine. It'll be enough to get the kitchen cleaned out and the rest of the cottage put in order."

"Here's the thing, though I'd like you to keep this quiet. I haven't been able to get in touch with the girlfriend—her name is Danielle St. Claire. I have reason to believe she was here the weekend before Mitchell died, but no one has been able to determine what happened to her. Apparently, she wasn't here when Mitchell returned from a speaking engagement, although they had planned to be together that weekend."

"Whoa! That's creepy!"

"Just keep an eye out for anything that strikes you as odd, a note or anything else that might suggest where she went. I didn't come across anything when I was here yesterday, but I was more focused on what to put where so the son, Timothy, would be able to decide what to keep and what to sell, donate or discard."

"Okay."

Gaby took Karen through the house together to orient her to its layout.

"I feel so badly for Timothy," Karen said. "I lost my parents when I was not that much younger than he is now. Devastating feeling."

"Oh? How awful! What happened?"

"Car accident. Mom and Dad were killed on the way to pick me up from summer camp. My younger brother was with them. He died too.

"There I was, totally alone except for an impatient counselor charged with seeing that no stragglers were left at the camp. I was getting angrier and angrier, thinking my parents had forgotten all about me, when Betty Browning arrived an hour or two after my scheduled departure time. She told me what had happened and bundled me up to take me back to Woodson Falls.

"Our families were close. I don't know what would have happened to me if Betty hadn't taken me under her wing and made me part of the family."

"Wow! How horrible to lose your parents and brother like that! And how very sweet of Mrs. Browning and her husband to rescue you and then take care of you. They had a number of kids, didn't they?"

"Six, actually. She kept saying that one more didn't make a bit of difference."

"Is that how you met Ken?"

"Yep. He was a couple of years older than me and pretty much ignored me until some guy in his class asked me to prom, and Ken told him, 'No way! She's mine.' We were practically inseparable after that. Who would have thought?"

"Sweet story. You been married long?"

"Six wonderful years in June."

"Congratulations!"

Karen poked her head into the upstairs closet. "You meant to leave these shirts and jackets here?" she asked Gaby.

"Yeah. I remember sorting through my husband Joe's things after I got out of the hospital. Ever read Joan Didion's book, *The Year of Magical Thinking*?"

"No. Never came across it."

"She talks about going into her husband's closet after he died, seeing his jacket, and thinking he must be coming home soon. While I never went quite that far, there was something about having a few of Joe's things around that kept him alive—even if only in my mind. I still keep a few of his shirts and his worn-out slippers, even after so many years have passed. Somehow makes me feel close to him again. Thought I'd give Tim the same option."

"I get it. I can't tell you how long I held on to my mother's nightgowns. I finally donated them to Goodwill, but having them mattered to me for a good number of years."

"I brought my dog with me. She's out in the car. I've been so busy with law work that she's feeling neglected, so I'm trying to take her along whenever I can. We'll be taking a walk along Donovan's Way.

I'll be back in, say, half an hour or so. Then I can answer any questions you may have and help you with anything that needs two people."

"Let me get to it. Enjoy your walk! It's a lovely day."

Chapter 24

As KAREN HAD COMMENTED, it was a lovely day. The air was a bit cool, especially with the breeze wafting across the still-chilled lake, but it was perfect for an afternoon stroll. Gaby leaned down to clip Kat's leash onto her collar. Neither she nor the dog was completely familiar with the area, which had limited open spaces, unlike the protected area around Gaby's cottage. There, she felt comfortable leaving Kat off the leash as they took their daily runs. All secured, the two sauntered down the roughly half-mile-long road toward Donovan's Cove.

Gaby had started bringing Kat with her whenever she could. Both seemed to benefit from the new arrangement. Accompanying Gaby meant the dog wouldn't be cooped up in the house for long stretches as Gaby's law practice became busier, especially with the notoriety generated by the Lakeview Terrace case. At the same time, having the support dog with her made Gaby feel more protected from threats to her safety and emotional stability—or both.

The houses along Donovan's Way were clustered in roughly the same configuration as when fishermen camped there. Most of the renovated buildings used the same footprint as the old fishing shacks. The cottages across the road from those directly on the lake took advantage of the gradual rise in the land, still able to capture stunning views of the water. The rise eventually ended in a sharp cliff that overlooked the collection of buildings. The presence of the looming rock face allowed these owners some latitude in using their lots. While still requiring variances granted by the quasi-judicial Board of Zoning Appeals, the properties' proximity to the cliff enabled their owners to enlarge the shacks a bit beyond their original footprint. The homes along that side of Donovan's Way were even closer to one another than those on the lakefront, similar to a suburban development but uncharacteristic for the rest of rural Woodson Falls.

As the pair strolled down the road, Gaby noticed a heron, looking much like a crippled old man as it stalked along the shore of the lake, hunting for dinner. The tang of the lake's waters was strong at this time of year, not yet in competition with the flowering shrubs that surrounded many of the cottages.

Approaching the end of the road, Gaby spotted a jumble of branches and grapevines ahead that was blocking the entrance to Donovan's Cove from the road. Winter winds had brought down the usual assortment of branches and tree limbs, which had to be cleared from areas like this that were a tangle of undergrowth. She thought the road crew would have been here already to clear out the area before summer residents complained about their access to the cove. Gaby wondered idly why they hadn't done the work earlier. There had been little snow to contend with this past winter, an unusual respite for both the full-time residents and the road crew. The mild winter had offered public works the opportunity to get an early start on spring cleanup in preparation for the busy summer season.

As Gaby turned to head back to 9 Donovan's Way, Kat pulled on the leash, directing Gaby through the branches and toward the still-frigid waters of Donovan's Cove. Gaby didn't want the dog playing in the water, knowing she'd have to deal with Kat's wet coat if she gave in to the dog's pull. She hadn't brought a towel with her on the walk and knew it would take Kat only a few shakes to cover Gaby in a cold, wet and likely dirty shower.

Gaby pulled Kat back with a firm "come" command. The dog seemed determined to ignore her. "Come now, Kat" Gaby repeated, but Kat plowed ahead, and Gaby was pulled reluctantly into the tangled branches and brambles, looking down at the ground to avoid tripping on a fallen branch or an exposed root and ending up in the water herself. Kat's low whine caused Gaby to raise her head.

There, mostly submerged in the waters of Donovan's Cove, with only the back bumper and part of the trunk visible, was a bright-red Honda Civic Si with a Quebec plate.

Gaby backed out of the warren of branches and vines that had been hiding the car from view, turned and raced back to 9 Donovan's Way with Kat close behind. Bursting into the cottage, the pair startled Karen, who was heading upstairs to continue with her cleaning.

"Is everything all right? You look like you've seen a ghost! Are you hurt?"

"No, no. I'm fine," Gaby panted, trying to catch her breath. "No ghost, at least not yet," she added, a watchful Kat leaning into her, tongue hanging out as she, too, panted after the quick run.

Going straight to the kitchen, Karen poured a glass of water and gave it to Gaby. Turning back, she searched the cabinets, found a bowl, and filled it for Kat.

"What's going on? Anything I can help with?"

"No, we're okay. Just found something I need to report to the trooper right away."

Assured the pair was recovering, Karen headed back to the stairs. "Call me if you need anything, okay?"

"Thanks, Karen. We're okay."

Gaby went into the downstairs bedroom, leaving Kat eagerly lapping up a second bowl of water. She had left her cell phone along with her purse in her car, so she used the bedside phone to dial the number for the resident state trooper's office.

"Woodson Falls Resident State Trooper, Matthew Thomas speaking. Can I help you?"

"It's me, Matt—Gaby. I'm calling from Mitchell's place, 9 Donovan's Way. I found a car—a red Honda with a Quebec plate—dumped into the cove at the end of the road."

"You sound out of breath."

"A bit. I raced back here to call you. I'm pretty sure I've stumbled onto St. Claire's car."

"I'll call this in to the barracks and meet you there."

"Whoever dumped the car into the cove pulled a mess of branches over the end of the road, probably to hide the car for a while. You might want to call someone from public works to come along to clear the area so a tow truck can access the car."

"Let me check out the situation first. This may require a call to the barracks for more assistance. Will you be waiting at the cottage?"

"It'll be dusk soon. Why don't I wait in my car at the end of the road? I'll pull over to the side and put my lights on so you will know where to go."

"Good thinking. Want me to deputize you now or later?"

Gaby laughed. "No, thank you. I just hope St. Claire isn't in that car."

"Or that it isn't St. Claire's car, which I seriously doubt."

"Right. See you in a bit."

Calling up to Karen, Gaby said, "I'm heading out to the end of the road with Kat to wait for the trooper. I found an abandoned car when we were out for our walk. It had been dumped into the cove. Might belong to the woman I told you about—Danielle St. Claire. You didn't come up with anything yet, did you?"

Karen headed halfway down the stairs. "Not yet. Women's clothes in the closet I'm assuming you left in there, and dried-out flowers, which I'm tossing. But like you, I didn't come across anything to suggest a woman was up here recently."

Gaby thought it best not to mention finding St. Claire's cell phone in Mitchell's office. "I'm not sure how long I'll be. I'd like to leave you a check for your work today plus a key to the cottage."

Karen came the rest of the way down the stairs. "Thanks for thinking of that, Gaby. It'll be fifty for today, but shouldn't Mitchell's estate be paying for this?"

"They will eventually, but it's going to take time for the executor to set up an estate account, and I don't want you to have to wait for a check. I'll bill the estate later for anything I lay out until the executor can manage things. In the meantime, I'm hoping you might pop by every two weeks or so to keep the place tidy until someone is living here and can make their own arrangements. Thanks for coming today and getting started."

Gaby left the cottage and got into her car with Kat. She wanted to get to the end of the road before Matt arrived.

Chapter 25

GABY JUMPED OUT OF HER CAR when Matt drove up and parked behind her. The light would fade soon, and she wanted him to see what she and Kat had found. Making their way through the branches that screened the road's entrance to the cove, they came upon the Honda. Its front end had been driven or pushed down an embankment and into the cove, the back end remaining on firmer ground. Once the branches blocking the entrance were removed, it looked like it would be relatively easy for a tow truck to pull the car from the lake.

"It's impossible to see what's inside the car from here," Matt said, as he snapped a few photos of the car and surrounding area, "or to release the latch to open the trunk."

"Just as well for now. I only hope we don't find St. Claire's remains in the car."

"At least then we'd know where she is," Matt quipped.

"That's not funny!"

"I got her plate number from the people up in Quebec," Matt said, opening the small notebook he carried with him. "It's St. Claire's vehicle, all right. I'm going to have to call this in. The State Police Dive team and possibly even Major Crimes will need to be involved with this. They'll manage the towing."

"Maybe they can confirm it's St. Claire's vehicle, just in case the plate was switched," Gaby offered. "Or there might be a clue as to where she is if her body isn't inside."

Matt led Gaby back through the brambles to his cruiser.

"Shouldn't we try to move the branches away?" Gaby asked Matt as he snapped more pictures of the scene.

"Nope. Police from the barracks will want to view this scene as we found it. In any event, once I've started the necessary files, I'll have to get back in there to see if anyone needs help."

"It's been a month since St. Claire disappeared," Gaby said. "She's probably beyond help at this point."

"But we don't know that for sure. The first step is always to search both the shoreline for anyone who might need assistance or first aid and, eventually, the lake for a body. I'm going to have to wait here for police from the barracks to take over the scene and determine next steps. I suspect Major Crimes will end up being involved with this, and they'll want to investigate this area for evidence of how that car got where it is," Matt answered.

"Can I help with anything?"

"Gaby, you look totally exhausted," Matt said. "Why don't you head on home with Kat while I start on the file to report a missing person as well as issue a Silver Alert, signaling an attempt to locate that person. Once I've got those started, I'll have to head back in there to begin a search of the shoreline. I'll let you know when police from the barracks get here and I'm relieved."

"That'll be very late, I suspect," Gaby said to Matt. "Want to come over for supper when you're done? I should be able to put something together for us to eat."

"Sure. That would be nice. I'll probably get to your place in an hour or two. Just need to get started on the paperwork after I call the barracks with an update and send them the photos I took, and before I head back through those branches to begin a search of the shoreline."

"Beer or wine? I don't have much in the way of liquor." Gaby asked when Matt arrived two-and-a-half hours later, spending a few minutes to get reacquainted with Kat before following Gaby to the kitchen.

"Either works for me. Which do you prefer?"

"I like wine either before or with dinner. Want to open this red for me? It's chianti. We're having pasta."

"Super." Matt grabbed the bottle and the corkscrew Gaby offered and eased the cork out of the bottle.

"There are two glasses over there," Gaby said, pointing to the island behind her as she stirred the pasta gently bubbling on the stove. The aroma of grilled vegetables cooking in the oven scented the kitchen. A mixed salad was on the kitchen table to the left of the island, along with a basket of sliced homemade bread.

"Smells great," Matt said, pouring some wine into each of the glasses and handing one to Gaby. "Here's to solving cases."

"Cheers. And let's hope we do," Gaby said, taking a sip of wine. "Find anything in your search of the shoreline?"

"No. The police team from the barracks arrived and will be continuing the search through the night. They're calling in the State Police Dive team, which will be out in the morning. Not sure if you'll want to be there. Even with the cold weather and the colder water, floaters can be a difficult sight."

"You think St. Claire ended up in the lake?"

"If her body's not in the car, which the dive team will be able to see before the vehicle is pulled out of the water, or in the trunk, once they're able to check that, where else would her killer dump the body?"

"I would think the trunk of the car is most likely. Certainly easier to transport the body from wherever St. Claire was killed down the half-mile to Donovan's Cove."

"I'm betting on the lake, possibly near the cottage even. Maybe wedged under the dock. That would be easier than moving her body to the trunk of the car. Either way, this long in the water would play havoc with any evidence that might be on the body."

"I guess we'll find out."

After taking another sip of the wine, Gaby drained the pasta then eased it into a simmering sauce, allowing the ziti to continue cooking while absorbing the sauce, which was fragrant with pesto. Once the pasta was cooked, Gaby spooned it onto two plates, then topped it with the vegetables she had taken out of the oven, drizzling some sauce over the pasta and vegetables. "Dinner!" she said, handing the plates to Matt, who put down his wine and carried the meal to the table.

"This looks wonderful! I eat too much restaurant food, but I'm too lazy to cook for myself. This is a real treat. Thanks!" He scooped up a spoonful of the grated Parmesan cheese Gaby had on the table, sprinkling it over the pasta.

"My pleasure. I enjoy cooking, but it can be a chore sometimes when you're the only one you're feeding. I eat my share of restaurant food too."

They ate for a while, then Gaby said, "I know we're assuming she's been killed, but what if she's alive?"

"That's what the search of the shoreline is about, though this long since her disappearance, I just can't imagine she wouldn't have turned up by now. I called Prescott Memorial like you suggested, but she was never seen there, and I looked at the ambulance run sheets to see if she'd been taken elsewhere but came up empty. It's not like she could hail a cab and leave Woodson Falls undetected. Someone would have run into her, or at least seen her. And then there's the cell phone that was left behind. No. I think the better odds are that she's dead and somewhere in the lake." Turning back to his dinner, he added, "This is delicious. Thanks again for asking me over."

They continued eating, chatting about the town and its residents. Then Matt asked, "I've been wondering. Why didn't you ever practice law in New York? I mean, you told me you have a New York license. Just seems strange. Can't have been easy to get both licenses."

"Actually, the states surrounding New York coordinate the test dates to allow candidates to sit for two state tests within a short period, but it's still three exhausting days, one right after the other. There's one multiple-choice exam that focuses on the common law, but each state also has an essay-style test geared to the unique aspects of that state's laws. Lots of writing."

"Why bother getting both licenses?"

"I went to law school at Columbia, and I wasn't sure what I wanted to do after I graduated. Taking both tests kept my options open. I maintain the New York license because Woodson Falls is on the border with that state and most of the part-time residents live in the city. It's come in handy, though my practice is centered mostly in Connecticut."

Chapter 26

MATT CLEARED THE TABLE once they were finished eating, placing the dishes in the sink. "Want help washing up?"

"Nope. I'll take care of it later. Let's finish the wine in the den," she replied, leading him to her favorite room. She put on some soft music and lit the logs she had set in the fireplace. Kat wandered in and leaned against Matt's leg, begging to be scratched on her head.

"Nice place," he said, sitting in the leather chair next to the loveseat. "Did you find it when you moved up here?"

"It belonged to my grandparents," Gaby said, sitting with her upper arm resting on the back of the loveseat, the left side of her face resting in her hand. "My sister and I stayed with them for a few weeks each summer while our parents were traveling to do research. Marcia—my sister—died of meningitis while I was still in college. My grandfather bequeathed the cottage to me when he passed away. I miss Marcia, but I'm happy to have the cottage."

"I'll say."

They sipped their wine, making small talk, then Matt asked, "What happened?"

"What happened when?"

"That scar you're trying to hide from me."

Gaby just stared at him as tears filled her eyes. Kat got up from dozing at Matt's feet and came over, putting her head in Gaby's lap.

"Mind if we talk about it?" he prompted. "It's really not that bad, you know. Surgeon did a great job."

"I don't know about that," Gaby began, taking a deep breath. "My husband—his name was Joe—had just landed a big advertising account, and we celebrated with champagne and dinner at our favorite restaurant. When we were walking home…" Gaby paused and got up to add a log to the fire, trying to hide the tears flowing down her wounded face.

"What happened?" Matt repeated softly.

"This tall man came at us with a knife. He stabbed Joe in the chest, then slashed my face. As I fell under Joe's weight, shattering my ankle, the man jumped into a white van and took off. Joe died before the paramedics arrived. The police never found the man who attacked us." Heading back to the loveseat, Gaby found herself turning into Matt's open arms.

Matt didn't ask questions they both knew she was ill-equipped to answer. He just listened as she told him that the senseless attack continued to prey on her mind, even after she had left her faculty position at Columbia to become an attorney. Even after she had moved to the cottage in Woodson Falls. Even now, years later, whenever she saw a white van with New York plates driven by a tall, dark-haired stranger. And Matt just listened, holding her close.

"Thank you, Gaby, for telling me. I didn't want whatever had happened to stand between us." Gaby just nodded into the warmth of his embrace until her tears subsided.

"I would have told you earlier, when we were in New York looking for Pieter Jorgenson and his truck a couple of months ago, but you had just told me about the senseless deaths of your wife, daughter and unborn child. My loss really pales in comparison."

"Still a loss. And you were there and hurt as well," Matt said, giving her a hug.

"It's past eleven," Gaby finally murmured. "You'll have to be up early to meet the dive team in the morning."

"Yeah. I best be on my way. You okay?"

"I'm fine. Thanks for coming over. Nice to have the company. And, honestly, thanks for making me get that off my chest."

"I'm glad. I really appreciated the invite—and dinner."

"I think I'll take your advice and stay in the office tomorrow morning. But do call me with any news about what the dive team does—or doesn't—find."

"Will do. Good night, Gaby."

"Good night, Matt."

Gaby smiled to herself as she cleaned up the kitchen. Matt was so easy to talk to, so comfortable to be with. So very understanding of what she had gone through when Joe was killed. Plus, Matt seemed content to let their relationship evolve at its own pace, which she truly appreciated.

Showered and dressed for the day, Gaby planned to work in her office. She skipped breakfast, not hungry after the late night dinner with Matt. The call she was waiting for from the trooper came in shortly after she sat down at her desk.

"The dive team just left," Matt reported to Gaby. "Came up empty. No body in the passenger compartment of the vehicle and nothing in the trunk once the car was towed to shore. The dive team checked further out into the lake as well as the waters of Donovan's Cove. Nothing. They're assuming the body washed out into the center of the lake, but the search of the shoreline is continuing with the help of some volunteer firemen who responded to our call. I'm headed out there to join them."

"Thanks for the update, Matt," she answered. "I agree, it's likely she's dead. But couldn't her body be somewhere other than the lake? Like on the cottage property?"

"But where? You said the only evidence of her even being at the cottage was the cell phone you found and the ingredients for the beef stew she planned to make for Mitchell, which, by the way, you can try on me sometime. You're some cook!"

"Thanks. Maybe I will, but you'll have to wait until fall. It's not exactly a summer dish."

"Seriously, though. If the body isn't in the lake, where would it be?"

"I'm thinking somewhere on Mitchell's property. It just makes more sense," Gaby responded.

Hanging up, she returned to the file in front of her but was too preoccupied with worry about St. Claire's whereabouts to accomplish much of anything. She decided to join the search, beginning with the grounds surrounding 9 Donovan's Way.

Heading to the cottage door, she called to Kat to join her and made her way to Mitchell's property. Arriving at the cottage, Gaby went into the crawl space and took one of the shovels resting against the stone foundation. She had decided to probe the wooded areas bordering each side of the property, isolating the cottage from its neighbors.

Off her leash, Kat had jumped out of the car after Gaby and trailed her to the back of the cottage, but quickly lost interest and headed for the dock.

Gaby began her exploration with the woods that ran along the driveway and continued down to the lake, looking for disturbed areas between the trees and places where the leaves looked arranged rather than having simply fallen from the trees or been blown there from the lawn. Where she found spaces of sufficient size to bury a human body, she probed the dirt with the shovel, looking for soft areas. Mostly, she hit ledge.

She crossed the property to the other side, pausing to take in the view of the lake. The water sparkled in the late morning sun, gently lapping the shoreline. A light breeze rippled the surface, which caught the light and shimmered like diamonds. The contrast between the deep blue of the lake and the lighter blue of the cloudless sky was broken only by the distant tree line and waterfall.

A pair of swans, swimming in synchrony across the lake, brought a tear to Gaby's eye. Swans mated for life, she knew. When one died, the other stayed forlornly alone. Was that her fate? Was she destined to remain alone over the coming years without the comfort of a harmonious, loving relationship with a spouse? Or was that her choice? She consistently rejected Bill Harrison's attempts to court her. Was she equally aloof with Matt, avoiding the possibility that their friendship might develop into something closer? Was she ready to take another chance at a lasting relationship? Another chance at love?

Katrina lounged on the dock, enjoying a nap in the sun while Gaby worked. She raised her head when Gaby moved toward the opposite woods and got up to accompany her. Working her way up the slight incline from the shore, Gaby continued to probe the ground, becoming frustrated with the futility of her efforts. Kat moved ahead, stopping at the outhouse. Approaching the structure, she began sniffing its edges.

"Smells from long ago, I think, Kat."

Kat turned her head when Gaby spoke, then turned back and began scratching at the outhouse door.

"Now what? Nothing in there, Kat."

The dog continued to scratch and began to whine.

"Here, Kat. I'll open the door for you to explore, but there's…" Gaby took a look through the outhouse door to see what might have piqued Kat's interest. A pair of legs were visible above the outhouse seat, the rest of the body stuffed into the depths of the hole, its further descent halted by the bulging belly of a pregnant woman.

Gaby turned and ran to the woods, collapsing on her hands and knees, heaving in an effort to empty her already empty stomach. Kat stood by her, whimpering at Gaby's obvious distress. Catching her breath, Gaby got up and rasped, "Gotta call Matt."

Closing the outhouse door without taking a second look inside, Gaby staggered up the hill, Kat at her side. When they got to the car,

Gaby pulled her cell phone from her purse, glad to see enough bars to make the call. She knew he had joined the shoreline search, so she decided to try his cell.

Matt picked up the phone after a single ring. "Woodson Falls Resident State Trooper, Officer Thomas. Gaby? Is that you?"

"Yes, Matt. I've stumbled onto St. Claire. You better get down here to Donovan's Way. And you might as well call Major Crimes again if they're not still here. She isn't missing any longer."

Chapter 27

"What do you mean? Is she buried somewhere on the property?"

"No. St. Claire's body was dumped—headfirst—into the business end of the outhouse."

"That's awful," Matt responded. "I'm on my way. I'll radio in to Major Crimes while I'm on the way. Where are you?"

"In my car. With Kat. Parked outside the cottage."

"I'll be there in a few minutes," Matt said, hanging up.

Gaby sat trembling in the car, hugging Kat to her. "Awful doesn't begin to cover it," she whispered to the dog. "Whoever did this must have really hated St. Claire—or felt threatened by her."

Matt pulled up a few minutes later. Gaby stepped out of her car. "Over there," she said, pointing across the property to the outhouse.

"You're shaking like a leaf," he said, giving Gaby a quick hug. "You sure you're okay?"

"It's a pretty horrific sight," she answered, "but I'm alright."

"Why don't you go into the cottage with Kat? I'll come in after I've checked this out. We'll need to wait for Major Crimes to arrive, anyway. Maybe we can unravel at least some of this puzzle. Provide some guidance for the investigation that's sure to follow."

"Okay," she answered. "Come on, Kat," she called, beckoning the dog out of the car and toward the cottage. "I'll leave the door unlocked," she called to Matt, who was already headed across the lawn toward the outhouse.

When he returned, he said, "I've seen some pretty bad stuff in the service and on the New York police force, but that… that's bizarre." He joined Gaby and Kat on the sofa in front of the massive fireplace in the main living area. Gaby had lit a fire against the chill that had seeped into her body.

"We don't know yet how she was killed, but that wasn't a random act," he continued.

"I know. It has to be someone who knew her—and despised her."

"Any ideas? People you think might be capable of doing that to another person? We can sort out how she died and who had the opportunity to kill her later. Somehow I think figuring out a probable motive may be the best way to narrow the field of suspects."

"I've been thinking about that since we found her car dumped into the cove. I was sure then that she was dead and kept wondering who might have killed her."

"And?"

"I can only think of four possibilities. People who could have a reason for wanting her dead. Of course, that doesn't rule out a stranger. When Rusty changed the locks for me, he found the door to the deck unlocked. Plus, a lot of people knew where Mitchell kept a spare key to the place. Still, it seems to me that dumping her body like that took a good deal of anger toward St. Claire as a person." She got up and poked the fire, adding a log. Sitting back down, she faced Matt on the sofa.

"Starting with those closest to her… Isn't that the approach the police always use? Suspect the spouse?"

"Most murder victims know their murderer, so yes, it's a starting point."

"So, according to his son, Mitchell was upset when he first learned St. Claire was pregnant with their child. Didn't want to get involved with caring for an infant at this point in his life. He was sixty-two.

She was in her thirties. Despite telling his son he was planning to ask the woman to marry him, he may have felt boxed in by the pregnancy. Getting rid of her was a solution."

"A pretty drastic one, though, don't you think? It's hard to reconcile wanting to marry someone with killing them, especially then disposing of the body in such a dreadful way. And killing your own child at the same time. That in itself is a pretty audacious statement."

"True. The son—his name is Tim—also said St. Claire wasn't pressuring Mitchell to marry her. Said she could raise the child on her own if that's what he wanted. Still, it's a motive, and Mitchell would have to be eliminated as a suspect."

"And he owned a gun. You said you secured it. Did you check to see if it had been fired recently?"

"How would I do that? And wouldn't there be some indication of a shooting somewhere in the house? I've been through this place several times. Even if Mitchell shot and killed her with a single bullet, wouldn't there be blood? Hard to cover that up."

"But not impossible. And she could have been shot outside. There's no one around yet to hear a gunshot. No summer people have come back to town. It's something to check out. You still have the gun?"

"Yes, it's secured in a locked drawer in my desk at home. It'd be an easy matter to turn it over to Major Crimes for testing if it turns out it was a bullet that killed her." Gaby took a deep breath before continuing. "Then there's the son, Timothy. Mitchell's will divides his estate between Tim and St. Claire. Three-quarters for Tim and one-quarter for St. Claire."

"Okay. Money is always a potential motive. I know you've met with the son. Any impressions?"

"Contrary to my expectations, Tim's a sweet kid. Very close to his father. Very fond of St. Claire, even. Said she was a lot of fun. I certainly didn't get any vibes suggesting jealousy when I talked with him. He seemed pleased his father was happy with St. Claire in his life. And he said he was looking forward to being a big brother. He was really concerned about how St. Claire would react to learning Mitchell had died.

"Plus, he seemed surprised when I told him Mitchell had named him as executor of the estate. He was also surprised at the size of his father's estate. I have the feeling Mitchell never got around to telling his son about his will. In any event, Mitchell would have had to draw up a new will if he married St. Claire. A marriage invalidates a previous will."

"I didn't know that."

"Yeah. You can't disinherit your spouse unless there's a prenuptial agreement covering the disposition of the marital assets. Mitchell drew up his present will, along with other estate planning documents, around the same time Tim suggested his father's relationship with St. Claire got serious. That's reflected in his decision to provide for her, even though they hadn't married yet."

"But isn't that another good reason for Tim to kill her? Get rid of her before his father could change his will? If she died before Mitchell, as you suspect happened, wouldn't her share automatically go to Tim?"

"Yes. That's the way Mitchell's estate plan is designed."

"Also, I'm aware that sometimes people who are beneficiaries of a will are envious of the share the other beneficiaries receive regardless of the size of their own share. It's a possible motive."

"Still, there's no way Tim could have known Mitchell would die suddenly, even though he had a history of heart disease. There was a phone message from Tim about visiting his father before the end of Harvard's spring term, which I think came in just before Mitchell had died. The heart attack couldn't have been anticipated. It could easily have been a long, long time before Tim would come into any of Mitchell's money."

"Okay. But we still have to consider the son as a suspect. Unlikely, but still a suspect. Who else?"

"Whoever killed St. Claire was enraged. And if her death occurred before Mitchell's, eliminating her would eliminate a threat of some kind. Mitchell's agent comes to mind, Alan Waterman."

"What would be his motive?"

"Tim told me St. Claire thought Waterman was charging Mitchell too much and not doing enough to promote Mitchell's work. Waterman might well think that St. Claire would convince Mitchell to find another agent. Given the popularity of Mitchell's books, it wouldn't be difficult for him to secure an agent who might agree to more favorable terms."

"Have you met this Waterman?"

"He was here over the weekend. Wanted to go through Mitchell's files concerning the book he was working on. I must say I took an instant dislike to the man, so that may be coloring my thinking."

"Your intuition at work again?"

Gaby laughed, "Never mess with a woman's intuition! But, apparently, Waterman and Mitchell had worked together for a long time. Since the first of Mitchell's books was placed with a publisher, Mitchell's relationship with Waterman had served him well. It's doubtful even the concerns of the woman he loved would have swayed Mitchell to drop Waterman in favor of another agent."

"Yet, Waterman wouldn't know that. Not for sure."

"But here's another possibility," Gaby continued. "If Mitchell had embraced the idea of having another child, he might have considered pausing his writing career, including his frequent speaking engagements, to be more active in raising this child and to spend more time with Danielle, who had a business and career of her own. An interruption like that would impact Waterman's income big time."

"There's a motive. Get rid of the potential spouse as well as the child in one fell swoop. Okay, that makes sense. So he's a suspect. Who else? You said you thought there were four possibilities. Who was the fourth?"

There was a knock on the door before Gaby could respond to Matt's question.

"Major Crimes. Officer Thomas? You in there?"

Chapter 28

MATT OPENED THE COTTAGE DOOR and went out to show the Major Crimes detectives where the body had been found. Gaby heard one of the detectives ask Matt, "Shouldn't you be out here, protecting the scene?" and Matt's answer, "I thought it appropriate to interview the individual who found the body. Besides…" before the voices drifted away as Matt and the Major Crimes team made their way to the outhouse.

Gaby knew it would be hours until the team removed the body from the outhouse, examined it before taking it to the morgue for autopsy, and finished with the crime scene. They'd want to question her before they returned to their base to file their reports and begin the process of solving the case. So she was stuck here in the cottage until then.

Her stomach rumbled. Despite the memory of St. Claire's lower body and pregnant belly emerging from the outhouse hole, which would haunt her for a long, long time, Gaby was hungry. Karen discarded all the old food in the house when she was here—just yesterday—to clean up the place. There were a few tea bags in a box on a kitchen shelf. That was it. *A cup of tea would be warm and fill up that empty space for now.* She put a kettle of water on the stove. While the water was heating, Gaby went into Mitchell's office to grab the two journals Tim had been interested in finding.

Taking her tea back to the sofa, then stoking the fire, Gaby began leafing through last year's journal. Perhaps Mitchell's entries would reveal his thoughts about Danielle's pregnancy over time, strengthening his motive for killing her or helping to eliminate him as a suspect. The detectives working the case could question others, but not Mitchell. Perhaps his journals could speak for him.

Going back to the December entries in last year's journal, Gaby found mostly thoughts related to the book he was working on. Scraps, really, of things he was considering he might include in the novel; turns of phrase that appealed to him and descriptions of the sights, sounds and smells of the frontier in which the Mohawk baronet operated. Interspersed were musings on Danielle and what life with her might be like.

He knew she loved her job and reveled in the business she had built from the ground up, as well as the interactions with people that enlivened her work. Interactions that had led to his meeting her and, ultimately, to their affair. She would be reluctant to leave Quebec and her business behind. He could write from anywhere, but did he want to give up the peace and quiet of Woodson Falls? Maybe it would be best to leave things as they were.

Still, he longed to know she was his, that she'd be with him for years to come, that in agreeing to marry him she felt the same way. Mitchell's yearnings and his love for St. Claire as expressed in the journal were hard to reconcile with killing her. And not much changed later in the month, following St. Claire's visit to Woodson Falls around Christmastime, when she told him she was pregnant.

Mitchell wrote about his mixed feelings: pride in his continued virility—that he was able to father a child at his age—while at the same time recalling those first several months following Tim's birth, when feedings and diaper changes disrupted the rhythm of his life around the clock. Then Tim's personality blossomed forth as he evolved into a real little boy, one Mitchell enjoyed and loved deeply. Could he tolerate a repeat of those early months for the sake of the years to come and his love for Danielle? Of course he could. It wasn't even a question when it came down to it. In fact, he wanted a different life for this child than he'd been pressured to have with Tim, with Eleanora urging him to agree to send Tim off to boarding school so he could concentrate on his writing and she on her design business. No, he'd want to be more involved in the daily life of this child, as well as spend more time with Danielle.

Gaby took a sip of her tea and got up to stretch. Carrying the cup of tea with her, she looked out the kitchen door window. The outhouse was visible from here. It looked as if the team was just bundling up St. Claire's body for transport. She wondered what they had found and how much they might reveal to her. Then she returned to the sofa in the main room and picked up the second, more recent journal.

This journal had a much different feel. Mitchell's now-familiar scrawl hadn't changed from December of the previous year to January of this one. And his thoughts concerning the book he was creating had the same tone as in the earlier journal, although he seemed focused more on character development than on scenic depictions.

But the many references to St. Claire, while still expressed in loving terms, had been circled with a different color pen. As January turned to February, that same pen crossed out her name in places, sometimes so vigorously as to tear the paper. Large *X*'s slashed through whole pages that were focused on St. Claire.

Gaby flipped to the last entry, written before Mitchell had left for Scranton. It said:

> Danielle is coming for the weekend!
> She'll be here when I return home
> from Pennsylvania. I've set flowers in
> our bedroom to welcome her. I've
> been carrying this ring with me for
> months now, and it's time to put it

> on her finger. I do hope she'll say
> "yes." I love her so very, very much.
> I truly want to spend the rest of my
> life with her, baby and all.

Gaby wondered whether Mitchell had taken the journal with him to Pennsylvania, since it seemed his practice was to journal every day. But there were no entries after this one, and this final page from the book looked scrunched up as if someone had tried to tear it out. Then the page had been flattened out, the small tear at the top taped.

Gaby recalled St. Claire being gone when Mitchell returned from his speaking engagement. He had called her Quebec office on Monday looking for her. Having decided to propose marriage, he had to have been distressed by her sudden absence. Yet he hadn't turned to his journal to puzzle out his thoughts as he had on earlier occasions. It seemed odd, Gaby thought, imagining the confusion and despair Mitchell must have been feeling. With no one with whom to share his thoughts, he'd naturally turn to his journal. But he hadn't. Could that be an indication that he had killed her?

When Eleanora stopped by the other evening to return the journals, Gaby assumed she had taken them when she was at the cottage following Mitchell's sudden death, which made sense with her saying she thought they might be useful in writing Mitchell's obituary. What if she had taken the journals earlier, when Mitchell was away? That would explain Mitchell's failure to write anything in this year's journal after he returned from Pennsylvania. Emma had remembered seeing Eleanora the same afternoon she saw St. Claire, while Mitchell was still in Pennsylvania. Could Eleanora have gone to the cottage then and taken the journals? But why was she in Woodson Falls in the first place? And why would she be so interested in the journals that she felt compelled to take them? Was it Eleanora who had crossed out St. Claire's name? Was she trying to erase the woman from Mitchell's life? So many questions and no real answers. None of it made any sense.

Eleanora was Gaby's fourth suspect, but her motive wasn't clear. She recalled Eleanora's agitation at the mention of Danielle St. Claire's name when they first met, and she knew from Emma that Eleanora had accused Mitchell of various infidelities. What was that saying? "Hell hath no fury like a woman scorned." After all these years, could Eleanora's jealousy of Mitchell's relationship with St. Claire have fueled her hatred to the point of murder?

A knock on the door interrupted her train of thought.

"Attorney Quinn," Matt said, "this is Detective Brendan Fisher of Major Crimes. He has a few questions for you."

"Glad to help," Gaby replied, shaking hands with the detective.

"Haven't we met before?" Fisher asked.

"I believe you're referring to the Jorgenson matter, up on Lakeview Terrace," Matt answered for her.

"Ah yes, that was a tough one," Fisher responded. "You go around town looking for trouble, Attorney Quinn, or does it follow you?"

At Gaby's startled expression, he added, "Just joking. So what's your involvement here?"

"I'm the attorney for the estate of the owner of this property, Phillip Mitchell. I believe the woman in the outhouse is Danielle St. Claire. I understand from the son that Mitchell intended to marry her. That was his baby she was carrying."

"That connected in some way to the Honda that we pulled from the water and brought to our base?"

Matt chimed in again. "Yes. Attorney Quinn and her dog found the car and called me. It belonged to St. Claire. We think it was dumped there to delay anyone from finding the body."

"Any idea when all this might have happened? The body's only partially decomposed, and I know the coroner would like some sense of the timeline in order to estimate the time of death."

"From what I've been able to piece together so far," Gaby responded, "sometime the evening of Friday, April 15. St. Claire owned a travel agency up in Quebec. Her office said she had planned to come to Woodson Falls that day and stay the weekend. Mitchell called the office looking for her the following Monday, but they hadn't heard from her. Is there any indication of how she died?"

"Coroner thinks she was strangled. The thyroid cartilage was crushed, possibly by a metal object that left diagonal indentations. Kind of like that fire poker over there, but not as smooth."

"Excuse me," Gaby said, heading to Mitchell's office. Matt and the detective followed. "Like this?" she asked, pointing to the fire poker hanging from the stand to the side of the fireplace. Unlike the one in the main room, the metal of this one had been twisted in a spiral design.

Chapter 29

"I THINK SHE WAS KILLED HERE."

"Huh?" Matt and Detective Fisher remarked in unison.

"Think about it. St. Claire left Quebec early in the morning the Friday she was killed. She had driven from Quebec to Saratoga Springs to scout out a location for a future tour she was planning. She spent several hours in the Saratoga area, visiting the sites as well as identifying places for tour participants to eat and, possibly, spend the night. She took off for Woodson Falls following her visit to Saratoga Springs, arriving here in the late afternoon. Once she arrived, she stopped at the grocery store to pick up ingredients for a stew she planned to make for Mitchell.

"We don't know when she intended to cook the stew, either ahead of time or after Mitchell came home. But I imagine she was tired. It'd been a long day, with a long drive, and I understand that a pregnancy itself can be fatiguing. She knew she would be spending the night alone at the cottage and may have decided to take a nap. I think she was sleeping on this sofa when she was strangled," Gaby continued, pointing to the leather couch. "I found her cell phone under the cushions when I was hunting for Mitchell's journals."

"That has a certain logic to it," Fisher said. "Anything else?"

"When I found her car, I expected her body to be in the trunk. That seemed to me to be the most efficient way of disposing of it, especially if St. Claire's killer didn't want to just leave her here. When the police divers didn't find her body in either the car or the lake, I kept thinking it must be somewhere on the property here at 9 Donovan's Way. It was my dog's curiosity about the outhouse that led to my discovery of her body."

"Attorney Quinn and I were discussing possible suspects while we waited for your team to arrive," interjected Matt. "She's interacted with the people closest to Mitchell and, because of her familiarity with the case, has some insight into possible motives behind this murder."

Gaby picked up the discussion. "Dumping her body like that suggests whoever killed her knew and despised her. The location the killer chose to dispose of the body is, in itself, a statement about how that person felt about St. Claire."

Fisher sat down at Mitchell's desk and gestured to Gaby and Matt to sit on the sofa. "So, what are your suspicions, Attorney Quinn?"

Gaby spoke first of Mitchell and his reaction to St. Claire's pregnancy as a possible motive to kill her. "But I've been looking through his recent journals and what he wrote there suggests he had come to terms with the pregnancy and wanted to marry St. Claire. He was in Scranton, Pennsylvania, for a speaking engagement the Friday evening I believe she was killed and planned to stay overnight, returning to Woodson Falls the following day. He could have returned early and killed her, but that can be checked with the people at the hotel.

"Mitchell certainly had access to the cottage and the strength to carry or drag St. Claire's body through the kitchen and to the outhouse. And he knew the area well enough to know where to dump the car. But based on his feelings for St. Claire as well as for their unborn child, as expressed in the journals, especially the most recent one, I think it's very doubtful he was the murderer. Plus, he called St. Claire's travel agency the following Monday, looking for her. I doubt he'd do that if he killed her.

"If he did murder her, his remorse might well have contributed to the heart attack that killed him several days later. On the other hand, his worry about where she might be could have the same effect. Of course, he can't be questioned, but his activities on Friday and Saturday can be checked."

"Makes sense," Fisher remarked. "Who else is on your suspect list?"

Matt spoke up. "The son, Timothy Mitchell, apparently stood to inherit a good portion of Mitchell's estate, but he would be sharing the estate with St. Claire. Money is always a potential motive but, according to Attorney Quinn, there's plenty there, although that doesn't always matter to an especially greedy beneficiary."

"But I didn't get the impression Tim knew he stood to inherit from his father or that he would be sharing the estate with anyone," Gaby added. "And he couldn't have known when his father would die. Besides, he seemed to be fond of St. Claire, was happy his father found someone he loved, and even seemed pleased with the thought of becoming a big brother to their child.

"That said, Tim did spend a good deal of time here when he was growing up and knew the area. I think he is physically capable of carrying St. Claire's body to the outhouse. He's a student up at Harvard. Again, it should be pretty easy to determine his whereabouts on the night St. Claire was murdered."

"Okay," said Fisher. "Anyone else on your list?"

"Two more. According to the son, St. Claire thought Mitchell's agent, an Alan Waterman, charged too much and didn't do enough to promote Mitchell's books. I met with Waterman over the weekend, and he certainly seemed to know his way around the place. There was a phone message from Waterman to Mitchell saying he wouldn't be able to attend Mitchell's talk in Scranton. That same message suggested Mitchell had invited him over for dinner while St. Claire was here and told him she would be at the cottage the prior evening.

"Waterman had been Mitchell's agent for a long time. Losing that relationship would have been a blow financially as well as hurt his reputation. He may have been sufficiently insecure to be concerned St. Claire would hold sway over Mitchell's decision, but that's a reach. Still, the entries in Mitchell's journal suggest that Mitchell intended to have an active role in raising the child St. Claire was carrying, which would likely throw a monkey wrench into his producing a new novel every two years, which seemed to be his practice. Having met Waterman, however, I'm not sure he would have the strength to move the body to the outhouse."

"Did you get any idea of where Waterman might have been on that Friday evening into Saturday?"

"His phone message said he had to attend a new author's book launch in Syracuse, New York. I'm sure his agency would be able to give you information to check that out.

"By the way, when the locks on the cottage were changed, Rusty told me the kitchen door out to the deck was unlocked. If I'm right about St. Claire being killed here in the office, that would be the shortest route to the outhouse. Whoever killed her was probably in a hurry to clean up here after dumping her body as well as to get rid of the car. I don't know if that's significant, but it's another piece of the puzzle."

"Okay. That's possible," Fisher said. "We can dust the doorknob for fingerprints. Who changed the locks? Hopefully, they haven't gotten rid of the old sets yet. We should have that person's prints for purposes of elimination, as well as your own."

"Rusty Dolan. I'll give you his number before you leave," Gaby said.

"So you've identified three possible suspects," Fisher continued. "Who's your fourth?"

"This is a stretch. Mitchell's ex-wife, Eleanora, was the person who contacted me first about representing the estate even though she had no legal interest in Mitchell's affairs or his assets. When I met with her, I explained that Mitchell's will would nominate an executor as well as identify beneficiaries. It turned out the son, Tim, was named executor and was the primary beneficiary of Mitchell's estate, with St. Claire given a one-fourth share in the assets, although I'm not sure Eleanora knew the terms of the will. I certainly didn't tell her. Besides, I'm sure St. Claire was killed before Mitchell passed away.

"The ex-wife's immediate concern was paying for her son's Harvard education, an expense Mitchell had taken on. Turned out he had set up a substantial 529 plan for Tim's education, though there would be no way for Eleanora to know that. Besides her concern for the costs related to Tim's schooling, I think she might have been intensely jealous of Mitchell's relationship with St. Claire. Would you excuse me a minute?"

Gaby went back to the main living area and returned with the journal she had been examining. "Mitchell had developed the habit of journaling as a kind of writing discipline, beginning years ago when he was working on his first novel. He was in the midst of his ninth book." Gaby gestured to the bookshelf and the line of journals there, identical to the one she was holding. "When I met here with Tim, he looked for the journals for this year and last and couldn't find them."

"Is this going somewhere?" Fisher asked.

"Yes. It turned out Eleanora had the missing journals. I thought she might have taken them the night Mitchell died when she was here to identify the body. And I believed her when she said she took them to write his obituary. But, take a look here." Gaby gave the journal to Fisher and pointed out the markings where St. Claire's name was written, as well as the partially torn page that had been taped back into the book. Matt came over to look as well.

"After I first heard from Eleanora, we met here at the cottage to find Mitchell's will. She became very agitated when I was reviewing Mitchell's file of legal papers and mentioned he had named St. Claire as his agent for healthcare decisions. I didn't think much of it at the time. I hadn't yet come across evidence that St. Claire was any more than a friend Mitchell trusted. But I have the feeling now that Eleanora was furious that Mitchell intended to marry St. Claire.

"A friend of mine at the grocery store recalls seeing Eleanora here in Woodson Falls the Friday that St. Claire was killed. It's about an hour-and-a-half drive from New York City, where Eleanora lives, to Woodson Falls. Yet my friend said she's seen the ex-wife pretty often, including that Friday. Makes you wonder why she kept being drawn to this area. She's a big woman, but I don't know if she'd have the strength to move St. Claire's body from here to the outhouse. Still, jealousy is a powerful motivator, and it's entirely possible…"

Fisher interrupted her. "That *is* quite a stretch. If we rule out the other three suspects you mentioned, meaning each of them has a verifiable alibi, we'll look into the ex-wife, but it's probably a long shot. Women who murder are a rare breed."

"One other thing," Gaby said. "Mitchell kept a spare key to the cottage behind the eave above the door, and apparently a lot of people knew that. So that opens the field of suspects even wider. Just a consideration."

Fisher put the journal down on Mitchell's desk and turned to Matt. "What do you think, Officer Thomas?"

Chapter 30

"ATTORNEY QUINN HAS PROVIDED US with a pretty good roadmap for identifying possible suspects and confirming their whereabouts on the evening in question," Matt responded. "I agree it would be wise to eliminate those before considering the ex-wife. I guess, like you, I have trouble imagining a woman, regardless of how jealous or enraged, doing something like this."

"Okay then. We're agreed. And thank you, Attorney Quinn, for your thoughtful contributions to solving this," Fisher said. "Major Crimes will be taking over the investigation at this point. If you're right about the murder weapon and where the victim was killed, this will need to be considered a crime scene. Do you need anything from the house for the estate?"

"No. I'm fine. I just want to make sure this fire is out before I leave. I expect you'll want a key to the place," Gaby said, handing over her key to Fisher along with Rusty's number. "I'll tell the cleaning person to hold off until your team is done with the investigation, and I'll have to call the son and let him know what happened to St. Claire."

"I expect that won't be an easy call to make," Fisher said, "provided he isn't the murderer and knows already."

"No, it won't be easy. Tim will be devastated by the news. I'm pretty convinced he didn't kill St. Claire, and I certainly hope I'm wrong about his mother being the murderer. On top of his father's death and now St. Claire's, it would be too much."

"Well, thanks for the key and taking the time to talk with me today," Fisher said. "Make sure you lock up when you're done here."

Matt accompanied Fisher to the waiting van he'd arrived in with the rest of the team. Gaby scattered the embers of the fire that had died down while she was talking with Fisher. Kat was asleep on the sofa in the main room.

"You still shook up?" Matt asked when he returned. "That was some sight in the outhouse. You did a great job of detailing the possible suspects. That had to have been hard after seeing St. Claire like that."

"Talking it out actually helped. Took me away from thinking about that outhouse and what it contained. But I'm ready to get out of here, just as soon as this fire's out and I can close the damper."

"I called into the barracks after notifying Major Crimes about finding St. Claire's body so Woodson Falls would have coverage while I was involved with this. I best call again to say I'm back on duty. I'm just hoping nothing big came up while I was here. How about I meet you at the café for an early dinner? You must be starving."

"I am. That would be nice. I'll need to head home first with Kat to feed her. I'll see you in a bit."

Matt was sitting in a booth when Gaby arrived a half hour later. Helen brought a coffee for Matt and herbal tea for Gaby.

"Guess we come here too often," Matt said to Helen, looking over the menu.

"I'm starved, Helen. I'll have the fish and chips," Gaby said, warming her hands on her teacup.

"Chicken pot pie for me, thanks."

"What a day!" Gaby said. "Thanks for staying with me at the cottage rather than guarding the scene of the crime."

"She'd been in there, what? A month?" he said. "And there's still no one around. At least, no curiosity seekers."

"It'll take a while for me to get that image out of my head."

"You can say that again. What was with the journals? You never mentioned them before today."

"They didn't seem all that important until today when I started to look at them while you were with the crime team." Gaby took a sip of her tea. "Tim wanted to read his father's journal from this year. I suppose it was a way to be close to him, now that he had died. That's when Tim noticed the two most recent journals were missing.

"Mitchell used journals as a way of thinking about his books as well as adding personal stuff, like his relationship with St. Claire. The earlier journals were on the bookshelf in the office, but the two Tim were interested in were missing."

"When did they turn up?"

"Like I told Fisher, the ex-wife, Eleanora, had them. She called me last Saturday evening wanting to get into the cottage. Practically threw a tantrum because I had changed the locks."

"She had them? Why?"

"She said she took them to write Mitchell's obituary. I assumed she picked them up when she was at 9 Donovan's Way the night he died. Eleanora was listed as an emergency contact at the hospital, and they had called her to verify his identity. But now…"

"You have doubts?"

Helen interrupted with their meals. Both dug in before resuming their conversation.

"Yes, I'm having second thoughts about when she took the journals."

"Why?"

"Mitchell was a very disciplined writer. He wrote a journal entry pretty much every day. But there's nothing in this year's journal past the day he left for Scranton. I can see him leaving the journal at home while he was in Pennsylvania for the speaking engagement, but when he came home? The woman he loved and planned to marry—the one who was carrying his child and who he thought would be at the cottage to greet him—was gone. Surely, he would have written something about that, trying to figure out why she might have left and where she might be."

"But he hadn't."

"No. That's why I think they were taken before he died." Fork in hand, Gaby said, "Let's finish eating."

When they were done with their meals, Matt said, "Did you notice that white powder on St. Claire's body?"

"No. Actually, I took one look and went into the woods to lose the breakfast and lunch I never had."

"The coroner with Major Crimes took a sample of the powder to test, but she thought it might be lime. Said that would be why there were few odors even though decomposition of St. Claire's body had begun."

"There's a bag of lime in the crawl space under the cottage. Nell Whitney told me lime is good for sweetening the soil. I thought it might have been used for the shrubs around the cottage."

"According to the coroner, lime has been used in mass graves to mask the odors. Some people think it hastens decomposition, but it doesn't work that way. It actually slows down the process."

"Hmm…"

"What?"

"I was at the cottage earlier on Saturday to meet Alan Waterman. Before he arrived, I took the time to explore the crawl space as a possible burial site. I left when I heard Waterman drive up, and I was sure I turned off the light and closed the door before going to greet him."

"And?"

Helen came to take away their dinner plates. "Anything else?"

"I'll have a slice of apple pie," Matt said. "Gaby?"

"Just another herbal tea, please, Helen."

"Coming right up."

"When I came back later that evening to secure the journals—Eleanora had left them in a plastic bag on the doorknob and rain was expected that night. Anyway, as I was leaving, I noticed a light coming from below the cottage. The door was open, and the light was left on. I also noticed a sprinkling of lime. I hadn't remembered seeing it before, but who knows? Anyway, based on what Nell had told me, I thought at the time Eleanora might be using the lime to keep the shrubs growing. Now I wonder…"

"Hmm… Seems like a good reason to keep her on the list of suspects."

"Yes. And maybe move her a little further to the top of that list."

Matt had to return to the office after their meal. He promised to keep Gaby updated with any new information regarding the case.

It hadn't taken long. Gaby was wrapping up her work a week later when Matt called with news.

"Mitchell and the son Tim were where they were supposed to be that Friday evening into Saturday. But Waterman wasn't in Syracuse that Friday, as he claimed. The book launch he told Mitchell he had to attend was scheduled for the following week. And you told me Emma had seen Mitchell's ex-wife the evening that we think St. Claire was killed.

"The Major Crimes detectives brought both Waterman and Eleanora in from New York for questioning, separately of course. Both waived extradition, each claiming innocence."

"Were they represented by counsel?" Gaby asked.

"Not right away. Both were Mirandized and each maintained the other was responsible."

"That's interesting!"

"Apparently, Waterman said that he had come to Woodson Falls to talk St. Claire out of the idea of marrying Mitchell, but that Eleanora showed up as well and ended up killing the woman in a fit of jealous rage.

"Eleanora said that it was Waterman's love for her that drove him to kill St. Claire. That he saw how miserable she was, even though she was divorced from Mitchell, and wanted to make her happy."

"That's crazy!" Gaby exclaimed. "That just doesn't make any sense!"

"Since when has a crime as heinous as this made sense?" Matt asked. "Anyway, Waterman gave it up after a few hours of questioning. He's the one who killed St. Claire, but Eleanora apparently did nothing to stop him and helped dispose of the body, so she's considered an accessory to murder. They both retained local counsel, but it's a bit late for that. Eleanora has the best chance of receiving a lower sentence, although the minimum sentence for murder in Connecticut is twenty-five years."

"Wow! Poor Tim... Loses his father, his mother, and a potential step-mother and sibling all in one dreadful act," Gaby said.

"And that's not all," Matt continued. "St. Claire was far enough along in her pregnancy for the fetus to be viable so, under Connecticut law, the murder of both mother and child is considered capital felony murder, which carries a life sentence. Waterman will definitely go to jail for life, but so may Eleanora."

Matt paused, then asked, "Have you spoken with the son about St. Claire?"

"Yes. He took the news of her death very hard. This has got to be worse, though, to have his mother locked away. Has anyone called him? Should I?"

"I don't know. It's a lot for a kid to absorb. If it was me, I think I'd want to know about the charges right away, but that's from the perspective of a cop with a lot of years of living. For a young man just entering adulthood? I just don't know."

Chapter 31

WHEN GABY CALLED TIM WITH THE NEWS of his mother's and Waterman's arrests, he had already heard. Eleanora had asked the attorney representing her to call him and explain the situation.

"Mother is looking for a plea deal. I guess the evidence against both her and Waterman is pretty solid, even though it wasn't her who killed Danielle. She was there and helped dispose of the body, which makes her an accessory. Apparently, that means she's equally guilty of the crime. Since both of them confessed, there's unlikely to be a long, drawn-out public trial. That would be hard to bear. All of this—losing Dad and Danielle, my brother or sister, and now Mother—it's just too much."

"Certainly is. How are you coping?"

"The people up here have been super-understanding. My academic advisor connected me with a counselor. She's been helping me to process all of this. She also reached out to each of my professors. I'm going to try to power through the summer session as I had planned, but I can take 'incompletes' if necessary.

"I decided to take a leave of absence come September and spend the fall semester at the cottage on Donovan's Way to try to work on Dad's book. I already talked to Dad's publisher about picking up where he left off. They jumped at the idea. I have you to thank for having planted the suggestion. And they're going to recommend a number of literary agents and intellectual property attorneys, one of whom might take Waterman's place as trustee of Dad's trust."

"That's good news. One more thing you won't have to worry about," Gaby commented.

"Yes. And if I do take that leave of absence from Harvard for the fall semester, there'll be no problem. I'm in good academic standing. But I'm hoping I'll be ready to go back in the spring."

"I'm sure you will be. You're a strong kid. Outside of the college, do you have any family or close friends you can lean on?"

"Dad's younger brother, Bill, has been a big support. He lives in Connecticut, not far from Woodson Falls. He and his wife Julie will be there for me if I need them. They were out of town when my father died, which is why the hospital ended up calling Mother. She was Dad's secondary contact. And then, there's you. You've been so good through all of this. You really tune into how I'm feeling, like you've been there, which you said you have."

"Yes, but everyone's different. I'm glad you feel you can reach out to me."

Their conversation turned to the memorial service Tim and his uncle Bill were planning for Mitchell and St. Claire.

"Danielle didn't have any relatives up in Canada. But she had told her relatives in Europe about her relationship with my father. They wanted her body cremated and buried here, with him. So that's what we'll be doing. I feel good about that.

"Weirdest thing is that Danielle named Dad as beneficiary of her life insurance policy. And her will left everything to him, including the value of her travel business. Because it's assumed that she died before Dad, her estate goes to him, and now to me. I'm rich, in terms of money that is, but so much poorer for losing the people I cared most about."

"So sad. Have you made arrangements for burying your father's ashes as well as Danielle's?" Gaby asked.

"Turned out Dad had purchased a burial plot a long time ago. It's in the Pleasantview Cemetery, just across from the road up to the Estates. It has a great view of the lake. You can actually see Dad's cottage from there."

"Once you have the details of the memorial service down, let me know. I'd like to be there."

"Of course. Hey, Gaby, thanks for the call. I'll get through this. Dad raised me to be my own person. He believed in me. Knowing that is a big help right now."

"I'm sure it is. Call me whenever you want to."

"I will. Goodbye now."

Epilogue

IT WAS NEARING THE FOURTH OF JULY, when the Woodson Falls Volunteer Fire Department organized a parade that involved most of the full-time residents, especially the various sports teams at Woodson Falls Elementary. They'd end the day with a fireworks display out in the middle of the lake that brought visitors from nearby towns.

Gaby sat in a booth at the Sunshine Café, leafing through a catalog from White Flower Farm. Summer residents were back in town, raising the noise level in the café.

Helen came over and poured coffee into Gaby's cup. "Same breakfast, hon? Two scrambled, bacon, biscuits, no potatoes?"

"Nope. Today it's blueberry pancakes."

"Bacon with that?"

"Of course."

"So, 'Mary, Mary, quite contrary, how does your garden grow?'" Helen asked, looking over at the catalog Gaby was leafing through.

"'With silver bells and cockle shells and pretty maids all in a row,'" Gaby recited, finishing the nursery rhyme. "Quite well, actually. I'm just looking to see what I might want to add if I end up with a few bare spots, which is better than the jungle I would usually be facing in another month."

"Good for you! Pancakes and a side of bacon, coming right up!"

"Thanks, Helen."

Helen came by with her breakfast a bit later, plunking a small pitcher of maple syrup down on the table as well as a dish of wrapped pats of butter. "Anything else, hon?"

"Nope. This looks great."

"Oh, my goodness. I almost forgot. Remember that tall stranger who was eating at the counter a while back? Said he was working on the old Haverson place?"

"Vaguely."

"You asked about him at the time. He's been in a few times. I didn't know much then, and I still don't. But he left this when he paid for breakfast last time he was in and asked me to give it to 'that lady lawyer.' I assumed he meant you." Helen dug into her pocket and pulled out a square white envelope, handing it to Gaby.

"That's strange," Gaby said, turning the envelope over. There was nothing written on it. "Thanks, I guess."

Helen left to wait on some newcomers. Gaby opened the sealed envelope and pulled out the white card. It was unsigned and read:

Joe wasn't who you thought he was. Better for you if you don't go down the same path.

"You okay, Gaby?" Helen asked, hurrying back to her booth. "You're white as a sheet! You need something?"

"No, it's just this message," Gaby stuttered. She laid the note on the table, her hand shaking. She could feel the anxiety mounting and wished Kat were here.

"Oh, Gaby. Just ignore it," Helen advised after reading the brief message.

"Easy for you to say," Gaby murmured. *Easy for you to say.*

Thank you for reading *Woodson Falls: 9 Donovan's Way*
If you've enjoyed reading this book, please leave a review on your favorite review site. It helps me reach more readers who may enjoy visiting Woodson Falls.

Subscribe to my newsletter at emeraldlakebooks.com/gabyquinn to be notified when *Woodson Falls: 2 Sunrise Trail*, the next book in the Gaby Quinn Mystery series, is released.

Author's Note

WOODSON FALLS: 9 DONOVAN'S WAY is a work of fiction. Just as *16 Lakeview Terrace* was loosely based on a probate case early in my second career as a small-town attorney, *9 Donovan's Way* was inspired by another case that left me with the uneasy feeling that I was missing something. And the description of the property and its cottage at the fictional 9 Donovan's Way emerged from a location I dealt with many years ago, playing a key role in how the story evolved.

After the struggles I encountered with *16 Lakeview Terrace*, learning to write fiction, coping with my husband John's deteriorating Parkinson's disease and eventual death, and dealing with my own disability resolved with an ankle replacement, I found penning *9 Donovan's Way* joyful. The writing flowed easily, and the characters came alive as I worked with them. And John still contributed to the story in his fascination with the French and Indian Wars, as well as in our own experience with a May-December marriage.

As with the first book in the series, this story is drawn in part from my experiences as an attorney specializing in elder law, estate planning, and probate issues. Also in play was a four-year term on my town's Planning and Zoning Commission, which informed much of the secondary storyline involving Pinkham's planned subdivision, Sunrise Hills.

All authors rely to some extent on expert input into a storyline. I am grateful to Sherman's Resident State Trooper Wayne Tate as well as retired state trooper and fellow author Marc Youngquist for their swift responses to my pleas for assistance. Their descriptions of how police procedure would play out at a critical point in the story without disturbing the basic plot placed *9 Donovan's Way* on better footing and enabled me to avoid an authorial *faux pas*. I am also grateful to Margaret Cook, who guides me in descriptions of all things related to dogs.

I am once again indebted to Tara R. Alemany, owner and founder of Emerald Lake Books, whose skillful editing and discerning eye suggested revisions to the manuscript that greatly enhanced the story and left me with the question, "Duh! Why didn't I see that?" I have grown by leaps and bounds as a writer thanks to her tutelage.

The creative insight of Mark Gerber, Tara's partner and the artistic force at Emerald Lake Books, was very much appreciated, especially in his brilliant design of the book's cover. Even more was his late recognition of a major flaw in my description of police procedure that led to a total revision of the manuscript. While my initial reaction was a "sinking tummy, toss it in the trash" feeling, recognizing the major work that was ahead, I am more confident of the storyline because of his questions and my search for answers.

I am equally grateful to my first readers: Terri Hahn, Ruth Byrnes, and Daria Romankow. Their early enthusiasm for this story, especially its characters, kept me going when I was drowning in necessary revisions.

As someone who enjoys cooking, I've had fun coming up with ideas for the food Gaby prepares for her friends. If you're interested, you can find the recipe for Gaby's shrimp and snap pea salad on my website at woodsonfalls.com/snappeasalad and her almond cookies at woodsonfalls.com/almondcookies.

It's my hope that you have enjoyed returning to Woodson Falls and learning a bit more about the town and its residents. I invite you to join Gaby Quinn on her future adventures as she continues to uncover what lurks just beneath the surface of this small rural town.

— Andrea

About the Author

HAVING RECEIVED A LIBRARY CARD before she began kindergarten (requiring her cursive signature), Andrea began her writing career at the age of five with a short story describing the seasons. Her next endeavor, at age nine, was a novella featuring Christine O'Leary. So began Andrea's long love affair with the written word.

Singularly focused on a nursing career, Andrea continued to write for pleasure throughout high school and college. After completing a master's degree to teach nursing, she was offered a position as a nurse editor with the *American Journal of Nursing*, where she honed her writing skills through editing others' works.

Andrea was in the midst of writing a novel styled as a memoir when her husband John's Parkinson's disease progressed to the point where he was unable to engage in his usual active lifestyle. He longed to "do something," so she suggested they write a book together. She had long considered writing a mystery series based on some of her experiences in her second career as an attorney, and they settled on one of her early cases as the basis for a book.

It was a great opportunity for both. Andrea had left a long career in a "publish or perish" university setting prior to becoming an attorney. It was hard for her not to view writing fiction as lying on paper. John helped her to push the uneasy feeling that was the seed for *Woodson Falls: 16 Lakeview Terrace* into a believable plotline. It was Andrea's long service as the chief elected official of a small town in Connecticut that provided the story's sense of place.

Andrea is the author of three award-winning texts in the area of nursing education and staff development, as well as numerous articles in peer-reviewed nursing and education journals.

Woodson Falls: 16 Lakeview Terrace was her first foray into the world of fiction, but it isn't her last. Having caught the mystery bug, she's intent on continuing with the Gaby Quinn Mystery series. To explore her books and learn more about Andrea's writing process as well as the backgrounds of people and places in Woodson Falls, visit woodsonfalls.com.

Andrea collects teddy bears and birdhouses, loves to garden and bake bread, and writes from Sherman, Connecticut.

If you're interested in having Andrea come speak to your group or organization about this book, the Gaby Quinn Mystery series, or about the writing process, either online or in person, you can contact her at emeraldlakebooks.com/oconnor.

For more great books, please visit us at
emeraldlakebooks.com.

Sherman, Connecticut

Made in the USA
Columbia, SC
04 June 2021

38987568R00114